The Red Road Home

The Red Road Home

HELEN IZEK

This is a work of fiction.
All the characters and events portrayed in this novel are fictitious products of the author's imagination. Any resemblance to real persons, living or dead, is purely coincidental.

Copyright © 2019 by Helen Izek.
All rights reserved.
Printed in the United States of America.
Published by Author Academy Elite
P.O. Box 43, Powell, OH 43065
www.AuthorAcademyElite.com

All rights reserved.
No part of this publication may be reproduced, stored in a retrieval system, or transmitted in any form or by any means—for example, electronic, photocopy, recording—without the prior written permission of the publisher, with the exception of brief quotations in printed reviews, nor may it be otherwise circulated in any form of binding or cover other than that in which it is published and without a similar condition.

Paperback ISBN: 978-1-64085-575-5
Hardback ISBN: 978-1-64085-576-2
Ebook ISBN: 978-1-64085-577-9

Library of Congress Control Number (LCCN): 2019932011

To my large and lovely family,
God's abundant gift to me

My heartfelt thanks to –

My husband, Ofer, and my children, Lee, Daniel, and Tamir, for your longsuffering patience and understanding as you quietly let me get on with the birthing of this book. It's been a while in the making—thank you for your support and for simply being the beautiful people you all are.

Kary Oberbrunner, the Author Academy Elite team and the Igniting Souls Tribe, for setting stellar standards for excellence, ethical service, and value. You are a unique and precious treasure trove of knowledge, guidance, wisdom, and encouragement for which I will be forever grateful.

Nanette O'Neal, for your patient, painstaking, and thorough editing and instruction. The lessons I've learned from you will serve me far beyond the covers of this, my first book.

My friend and sideline cheerleader, Debbie Hemstreet, for your prayers, advice, and valuable input. I would have given up on this particular project a long time ago if it hadn't been for you.

My parents, Russell and Anne Wyatt, for understanding and instilling in us, your clan, the importance of family. What an inspiration you both are.

My brother Brian, whom I will always miss, for teaching me not to take myself too seriously.

And last but not least, my own sisters, Liz, Sheila and Julia, for your interest in this project, your ongoing support and prayers, and for being the golden threads in the fabric of my life.

"You can kiss your family and friends good-bye and put miles between you, but at the same time you carry them with you in your heart, your mind, your stomach, because you do not just live in a world but a world lives in you."

Frederick Buechner

Part One

"Don't believe an accident of birth makes people sisters or brothers. It makes them siblings, gives them mutuality of parentage. Sisterhood and brotherhood is a condition that people have to work at."

Maya Angelou

Chapter 1

Paddy Maguire drove his jeep faster than usual down the last stretch of road towards home. The rainy season was over in this part of Africa and a cloud of red dust billowed in his wake. It had been a challenging day and he was tired.

"We're getting too old for this, aren't we Rex?" he said, glancing at the German shepherd dog on the seat beside him.

The dog whined as if in agreement as Paddy brought the vehicle to a grinding halt in front of a Spanish-style farmhouse. He always thought it looked especially beautiful at this time of day, sprawled against a backdrop of enormously tall trees and bathed in golden, late-afternoon light.

Tossing his hat and keys onto the lobby table, he headed for the bathroom to wash the grime of the day off his hands, and then out onto the verandah towards the noises of splashing and boyish chatter.

"Beth?"

"We're here, down by the pool," Beth called.

Paddy strode across the lawn and down a few rock steps to the pool-side *lapa*, Rex close at heel. Making a mental note to check if the thatched roof needed repairs after the rainy season, he ducked under its overhang.

Beth lifted her face and smiled as he placed his hands on the arms of her chair and looked down at her.

"Hello my darling, how's your day been?"

"Good, thanks." Beth's eyes crinkled into a smile as he kissed her soft cheek.

"And how's my growing girl?" he asked, turning to his daughter. "The Piglet behaving itself?" He planted a kiss on her forehead.

Becky cradled her swollen belly and smiled contentedly. "Kicking up a storm, so yes, absolutely. Please can you get the boys out the pool, Dad? They'll be turning blue with cold just now."

Paddy scooped up the towels from the stool next to Becky. "Come on boys, time to get out." He made his way down a couple more steps onto the stone paving surrounding the large swimming pool. "Gran's got a plate of jam and cream scones waiting for you."

"Coming Grandpa," said the taller of the two boys from where they stood on the highest ledge of the rock formation at the far end of the pool.

Paddy grinned as his two young grandsons simultaneously whooped and launched themselves into the air, knees tucked up and circled tightly by thin brown arms for the ultimate splash as they bombed into the water. They popped up like corks and swam with easy strokes to the rough-hewn rock steps at the *lapa* side of the pool. After a quick towel-down, they cupped the steaming mugs of tea with slightly shaking hands.

"Thanks Gran."

"Look at you, Ben," Beth said. "Your lips are quite blue with cold."

"No, Gran, I'll be fine in a moment. Not cold really. Promise." The elder boy sat down on the stone paving and blew into the mug before taking a noisy sip.

"Ben, we don't really want to *hear* you drink your tea," his mother said gently. "Riley, come here darling." Becky drew her younger son down onto the lounge bed beside her. She rubbed the towel vigorously up and down his boy-thin arms before giving him an affectionate squeeze.

Having drunk and eaten their fill, the boys pulled on their T-shirts and ran off to the far side of the garden to play football.

Paddy felt a strong sense of déjà vu. Many familiar scenes, long ago but not forgotten. How the years have galloped by at the most ridiculous pace, he thought with a deep sigh. Catching sight of Beth's concerned glance in his direction, he smiled reassuringly. "They'll work up a sweat, those two, and then be begging for another swim."

"No doubt," Becky said. She didn't seem overly bothered by his dire prediction.

Paddy stirred sugar into his second cup of tea and watched Beth as she settled back against the cushions of her chair. He wondered at the serenity of her beautiful face, almost unlined except for the crinkles around her eyes that deepened as she smiled.

"We're so blessed to have you living in the area, Becky darling," Beth said. "It's wonderful to have you and the boys so close by and to be able to be a part of your lives."

"Mum? What brought that on?" Becky frowned. "Are you alright?"

"Yes of course I am. I just suddenly realized how blessed we are. Aren't we, Paddy?" She didn't wait for an answer. "But I'm worried about your sisters. I don't think they've spoken, really, for years. It's awful, and I have no idea how to fix it."

The golden peace of the evening Paddy had felt so keenly a minute ago vanished. He realized that Beth was close to tears, as she always seemed to be lately when she mentioned Lori and Carla.

Becky noticed too but said nothing and laid a protective hand on her swollen belly.

"Do *you* speak to them, Becky? Do they ever speak to each other?"

"I do, actually. Every few weeks or so," Becky said. "One of us calls or messages the other. But it's always me with Lori, or me with Carla. I really don't know if they have any contact between them. In fact, I'm pretty sure they don't." She paused. "It's sad. I don't understand it. I don't know how or why it got like this. Or was it always like this, ever since Carla was born? What happened between them? I seriously can't remember."

Paddy didn't answer. He watched as Beth stroked her old Staffordshire bull terrier. Unable to bear the sadness that now shadowed her eyes, he turned away to stare out across the pool instead. Suddenly the noise of its waterfall seemed thunderously loud. A frog croaked, and then another, indicative of the sinking sun and lengthening shadows.

"It's not right, Paddy. We have to do something to fix it," Beth said.

"You're right, I guess," Paddy said, turning back to face her. "If there's a rift in our family, we shouldn't ignore it. Leaving the status quo is not who we are, is it?" Things had been so pleasant a moment ago. What had sparked this mercurial change in Beth?

"Are you making fun of me, Patrick Maguire?" Beth said, sounding irritable.

"No, of course not. I mean it," Paddy said, surprised at being misunderstood. "Of course I agree that this bad feeling between Lori and Carla has gone on for long enough and has to stop. It's not what we want for our family, and it's certainly not a good example for our grandchildren. I mean, for goodness' sake, they're grown women already. Why can't they just talk to each other?"

"Why should they? They never see each other," Becky said, pragmatic as always. "Easy when you live on different continents."

"So, we'll just make sure they do see each other again," Beth said matter-of-factly.

"What do you have in mind?" Paddy didn't know whether to feel relieved at the upswing in his wife's mood, or even more confused.

"Well," Beth began with a tone of steely determination in her usually gentle voice, "let's send them an invitation they can't refuse."

"What on earth do you mean by that?" Paddy asked.

Beth beamed at him. "It's my 65th birthday next month dear, and I think it's about time you threw me a party."

"But you loathe parties, Beth. You never let us make a big deal out of your birthday." Paddy was incredulous.

"Well, I want you to now," Beth exclaimed.

Paddy looked out over the pool and garden he and Beth had planned, planted, and cultivated together—beautiful in the soft light of an early African evening—labors of love for each other and their family. Their home and farm had seen hardship and prosperity, deep sorrow but also much joy over the more than forty years they'd lived there. He understood where Beth was coming from: it all meant nothing if their family was broken in some way.

He turned to Becky. "What do you think?"

"You know me Dad, Peacemaker Patty—isn't that what you used to call me when I was a kid?" Becky grinned up at him. "Seriously though," she continued, "I hate to see this bothering you both so much, so, I think it's a brilliant idea. If anyone deserves a party, it's you, Mum. And besides, it'll be great for us all to be here again. I think the last time we were *all* here at Kalulu together was for my wedding."

"Okay then," Paddy said slowly. He was still surprised but willing to do anything if it would help take the pain out of Beth's eyes. "You'll have your birthday party my darling, if that's what you want."

"It is," Beth said.

He squeezed her outstretched hand and knew that any effort on his part to make this happen would be worth it.

"I'll email or call them or something this evening," Beth chattered on. "Oh, and I'll ask Mae as well. She can come out a little earlier this year than originally planned. I'm sure that won't be a problem. Come on, Paddy, let's get these tea things in, before the mozzies give us a dose of malaria."

"You'll never guess what elaborate plan Mum cooked up today to try make peace between Lori and Carla."

These late-night oases of tranquility with Joe were a favorite time of day for Becky. The boys were long in bed and all was quiet.

Joe sat at the far end of the same couch with Becky's manicured but slightly puffy feet resting on his thighs. "Do tell." He grinned.

"A birthday party."

Joe stared at her. "What? She's never agreed to have anything more than a bit of a bigger tea for her birthday."

"I know. Crazy, huh? She's suddenly freaked out about them not getting along and is determined to fix it, poor darling."

"When does she want to have the party?"

"In a few weeks, I guess. Her birthday's in April."

"D'you think they'll come?"

"No idea. We'll have to wait and see, but if they do, it's going to be an interesting time, to say the least."

"And you just won't be able to keep out of it, hey? You'll be in the thick of it, right there with your Mum, trying to make it all right again," Joe said.

"Don't tease. It's serious stuff. I failed dismally to make it right when we were growing up, and since Lori left home, it kind of stopped being a burning issue." Becky sighed as Joe rubbed her feet. "I've always hated it, knowing they don't get on or don't have anything to do with each other. It's always been there, hovering in the background, but I guess it faded into the status quo, a mere fact of our lives." She frowned and shook her head. "But I guess Mum and Dad don't feel like that."

"Can't say I blame them," Joe said. "We'd hate it if our kids couldn't stand each other's guts."

"I know. That's exactly what I felt when Mum and Dad were talking about it this afternoon. It's a horrible thought."

They were quiet for a few moments and Becky became conscious of the operetta of shrieking crickets and rhythmically croaking frogs outside in the garden. Joe seemed deep in thought. She never tired of looking at him and her mind wondered back to when they'd first met at a mutual friend's sixteenth birthday party. He came from a large farming area several hours' drive south from where she'd grown up. With a daredevil attitude and good looks to match, he'd quickly stolen Becky's heart. To the surprise of both sets of parents, their teenage romance had weathered the tests of time and long periods of separation enforced by the fact that they attended different boarding schools.

They'd married straight after Joe finished his agricultural degree and Becky her art degree in South Africa and returned to Zambia to start their lives together. With some help from both sets of parents and a lot of hard work, they'd realized their dreams and bought a farm not far from her parents.

Becky's reminiscing screeched to a halt. "I feel bad," she said. "I've been so busy being a happy wife and mom, with the boys and our beautiful home, I've kind of pushed Lori and Carla's problems to the back of my mind. Is that awful?"

Joe frowned and shook his head. "Don't beat yourself up about it, Becks. You've been living your life. We've been busy here. It's been a hectic ten years, remember? And in any case, it's not your responsibility. They're big enough to take care of their own problems."

"Still . . ."

"Still nothing." He tapped her feet as if to signal the massage was over. "Come on, come to bed. You're tired. Stop shouldering the world's problems."

"Not the world, just my family's," Becky said. Yawning, she took Joe's outstretched hand to help heave herself up off the couch. "Jake'll be pleased if Carla comes up."

"Ja, I guess so." Joe switched off the lounge light and they walked hand-in-hand down the bedroom wing passage. "It's about time those two got their act together, one way or the other. I really don't understand why they haven't until now." He opened first one door and then the other as they looked in on their sleeping boys. "I'm glad we didn't wait around," he whispered.

"Really? You wouldn't have preferred to enjoy a few more years as a bachelor-in-demand?"

Joe grinned then shook his head. "No ways. Somehow, I'd managed to win the best, so I had to seal the deal before she got away from me."

Becky stood on tiptoes to kiss him softly. "Charmer. You always know how to say just the right thing. Now come on before we wake them up, or else I'm not going to get myself or the boys to school on time."

"I wish you'd stop working already," Joe said as he headed through the open door of their en-suite bathroom.

"Couple more weeks, that's all. I'll see this term through and then stop for the holidays."

Becky loved her job as an art teacher in the neighborhood school where Ben and Riley were pupils. She was also deeply grateful that it was relatively close by—convenient for herself but it meant that her children didn't have to go away to boarding school as she and her siblings had done from a very early age.

She gazed at her husband's reflection in the mirror as he brushed his teeth, planted a kiss on his bare shoulder and padded off to bed, still feeling a little guilty about how happy she was.

"So blessed," she murmured sleepily to herself as she sunk against the soft cool of her pillows.

Chapter 2

Lori had the dream again.

She was flying, like a bird. She struggled to breathe as she looked down from an impossible height but the cool air pushed against the fear as the breeze gently caressed her hair and face.

Soon she began to get the hang of it, even enjoyed it. She dipped her head and tilted her arms to dive down towards the green-brown land rushing beneath her—tall bush grass, open fields dotted with fat brown cattle, tree-covered hills, clusters of small mud huts and brick houses, smoking coal-fires—and then back up into the empty, pale blue sky.

A fish eagle flew up alongside her. She turned to look at the magnificent bird with its massive wingspan and upturned wing-tip feathers. Its eyes showed no surprise to see her there. It seemed to dip its noble, white-feathered head in acknowledgement as they flew together, comrades in flight. And then, with a haunting cry, it was gone.

Lori looked down at the long, dark red ribbon of road far below. Half-way along its length the road disappeared beneath a canopy of large dark green trees, re-emerging as a hump-back stone bridge over a shallow, glistening stream. Three children were playing and laughing on the bridge. She swooped down for a closer look.

Suddenly, she was no longer bird-like, no longer flying; she stood aside and watched the children play. Busy with their game, they didn't notice her. Each child had a pile of sticks and twigs that they threw over the side of the bridge on the count of three. Dashing to the other side of the bridge, they'd fling themselves down and peer over the edge, pointing and shouting encouragement to their respective wooden vessels as they reappeared, carried along by the stream's current. *Poohsticks*; Lori recognized the favorite childhood game.

The blond boy threw a stone with deadly aim at his opponent's stick as it came into view from under the bridge, snapping it in two and so ending its race.

"Hey! Come on, Jake," the dark-haired boy shouted. "That's cheating."

The two boys leapt to their feet and wrestled but she knew it was just a game. Sure enough, the boys broke away from each other, laughing, and raced back to the starting post where the girl waited for them, stick held at the ready for the next race. It was all so familiar . . .

"One, two, three," the girl yelled. "Ready or not."
"Wait for us, Titch."

Titch. That was the nick-name her brother Tom and best friend Jake used to annoy her; she wasn't *that* much shorter than them.

"You better wait, or I'll sink your ship next time," Jake said with a cheeky grin as he skidded into position next to the girl.

But the dark-haired boy didn't join his friends; instead he stopped in front of where Lori stood. He looked directly up at her and she stared back as if to absorb every detail of his dust-smudged face.

"Hello Tom," she said somewhere deep inside her.

He smiled his beautiful smile. "Hello Lori," he answered in a gentle voice that was no longer that of a child.

And then, just like the eagle, he was gone. It was all gone, and she was awake and alone in the dark, desperately trying to hold on to the dream, to Tom's face, the sound of his voice. But they faded relentlessly away, leaving her with nothing but salty tears making warm tracks down her face.

Gradually, Lori's tears dried and her breathing returned to normal. She could hear the twittering of early-morning birds outside so knew it was at least dawn. Easing herself quietly out of bed, she started in the direction of the bathroom, catching her knee on the wooden corner of the bedframe with a blow that made her gasp.

"Ow, oof. That's going to bruise," she muttered to herself as she rubbed it vigorously.

The man she'd left slumbering in the rumpled, king-size bed stirred and turned over. Her husband was a deep sleeper; she'd have to scream out loud before he woke up. Just as well, she thought, as she got ready for her morning run.

The other bedroom doors were firmly shut; it was an hour before the kids had to be up. She'd have time for a run and perhaps even a cup of tea in the garden before giving in to the demands of her daily routine. Luna, whom the family had brought home from the dog-pound a few years previously as a puppy of no distinct breed or origin, was ready and waiting by the door, trembling in anticipation.

Lori stretched and twisted before setting off at a comfortable pace down the single-track dirt road beyond their back garden, Luna bounding just ahead. The track took them out of the moshav where they lived and past the neighboring kibbutz.

It was early spring, Lori's favorite time of year in Israel where she'd lived for the last twenty years. The roadside grass and bushes were freshly washed from the recent rains and the air was clean and crisp. As a pale sun rose from behind the Carmel mountain range on the eastern horizon, a promising blue tinge seeped into the grey dawn sky.

Lori veered off onto a smaller path that cut through the fish farm and wound its way westwards to the coast. A small flock of flamingoes squawked and squabbled on the last pond she passed before jogging up the rise overlooking one of the many bays stretching along the picturesque coastline. Trotting down onto the white, sandy beach below, she found a stick and threw it for Luna who was after it in a flash, barking ecstatically.

While the dog retrieved the stick, Lori went down to the water's edge and watched the waves, sucked out and then thrown back against the rocks with a hiss of spray—an eternal, hypnotic rhythm of pull and thrust. God sets the borders of the seas, she mused.

Luna dropped the stick at her feet and nudged her leg with a wet nose.

"Once more, girl, and then we have to go back."

She laughed out loud as the dog took a couple of pouncing leaps into the surf to retrieve the stick, and then suddenly felt apprehensive about leaving all this behind. In another two days, she'd be on her way to her parents' farm in Zambia, Central Africa. She was excited to be going and knew that once she was there, she'd find it hard to leave again. But right now, this was her life, and she never felt wholly comfortable to pack up and leave it behind.

It was always the same, this heartfelt tug-of-war. But this time it was worse, as she was anxious about leaving her husband, Yoni, and children, Jonathan and Noya, behind.

Jonathan . . .

Panic jabbed in the pit of her stomach and started to twist its way up to her chest. The tears that never seemed to be far away these days stung her eyes as the thought of her son's upcoming army duty came rushing to the forefront. There had been violence recently, a terror attack in the Old City of Jerusalem and a random stabbing elsewhere. The situation was tense. Lori pressed her hands to her chest and breathed deeply, trying to gain control of her emotions.

"I will *not* be afraid, I *won't* live in fear," she repeated to herself until she felt calm again. She wasn't word perfect in the theology behind it, but she'd come to feel lately, somewhere deep inside her, that she had to resist fear—not only repress it but to uproot and throw it out. She'd become convinced that doing so could even be a matter of life and death.

Whistling Luna to her side, she turned her back on the brightening waves and her thoughts to her upcoming trip as she jogged back home. Her mother's call two weeks earlier had surprised her. While she'd always made a great fuss of everyone else's birthdays, her mother had never wanted to celebrate her own in any special way. Now here she was, planning a full-blown garden party.

"It'll be fun, Lori," Beth had said. "You must come."

"Mum? Are you alright? Is everything okay?" Lori wasn't buying this strange invitation at face value.

"Yes of course darling, don't be silly. I just miss you, miss you all. We haven't been together as a family for over ten years—since Becky's wedding in fact. So, I've decided this is an excellent opportunity. It *is* my 65th, after all," she'd finished, sounding a bit put out.

Lori, albeit skeptical, was sorry she hadn't sounded more enthusiastic and decided to accept the unlikely explanation.

"Well, if that's all it is, then I'm all for it, Mum. You deserve a good celebration more than anyone. We start our school holidays in a couple of weeks so if the dates are right, it might work. I'll have to talk to Yoni first, though, and the kids."

"They'll come with you, won't they darling? Noya and Jonathan at least. We haven't seen them since our last trip to you over a year ago."

"I'm not sure, Mum. They've got things going on, and this is really short notice. But I'll speak to them and let you know. Okay?"

Yoni had always been understanding of Lori's need to go back to her childhood home every now and then. It didn't happen very often; tickets were prohibitively expensive but he always came through when it mattered. Even as she'd spoken to her mother, Lori knew he probably wouldn't be able to join her, certainly not for three whole weeks; it was a busy time of year on the farm. Hopefully the kids would be free and willing to make the trip with her.

But they weren't. Jonathan, nearly 18 years old, would be busy with try-outs for army units and studying for his final school certification exams. And 16-year-old Noya had already committed to help out in the moshav kindergarten during the school holidays.

"I'm sorry *Ima,* but they're counting on me," Noya had explained. "I can't let them down now."

"I really don't want to go on my own and leave you all here."

"You can't disappoint Gran, *Ima,*" Jonathan had said. "You have to go. We'll be fine and you'll have a good time."

Yoni had hugged her close. "*Metuka sheli,* sweetheart, you go and have time on your own with your family. It's important for you. And if we can, we'll come join you. I can't promise but we'll try. And if we can't, then another time. *Beseder?*"

"No, it's not okay at all, but I guess I don't have a choice, do I?" Lori had replied, her voice muffled against his chest.

"No, not really. But you'll have a great time without us. A real holiday."

And that had been the end of the conversation. Lori tried to be optimistic. Perhaps they would come for part of the time, at least for the week of the party.

As she cooled down by walking the last hundred meters home, tasks and shopping lists spun through her mind. It was going to be an exhausting couple of days. She glanced at her watch and sighed as she pushed open the garden gate; no time for morning tea.

"Come on kids, hurry up," she called, knocking on the still-closed bedroom doors. "Last day of term. We can't be late."

As a teacher at the same high school her children attended, Lori shared in the end-of-term excitement of ceremonies, certificates, final meetings, classroom-cleaning, and farewells. The remaining hours of her days were filled with last-minute shopping, packing, house-cleaning, and cooking to fill the freezer for the family she was leaving behind.

And then it was time to say good-bye. She cried when she hugged Luna and left her with sad brown eyes behind the garden gate, and she cried again when she left Yoni and the children in the airport. She was hopeless at saying good-bye. Always had been. She blamed having to go away to boarding school from a young age and then living abroad, far from family and friends.

Standing in the queue for the security check, Lori turned back to wave until she couldn't see them anymore, and then, tears dried, she surrendered to a growing sense of sweet anticipation.

She was going home.

Chapter 3

Carla tapped her fingers on the steering wheel and hummed the tune playing on the early morning radio show. She felt relaxed, even while sitting in a bit of a traffic jam. This is the magic of Cape Town, she thought, rolling down the window to smell the sea breeze and hear the seagulls' cry as they rode the winds.

Maneuvering her old VW bug—a treasured remnant of her student days—away from the seaside neighborhoods and toward the youth center in the city's downtown where she worked, Carla thought about the trip she'd be making in a couple of days.

"Come on, sweetheart," her father had wheedled, "it's your Mum's 65th birthday. It's a special occasion and we want you here with us."

"I don't know, Dad. I wasn't planning on taking any leave right now." She'd made a half-hearted attempt to push back.

She knew very well why Paddy was the one who'd made the call; Carla never could resist her father, but the feeling was mutual. They were putty in each other's hands, wound around each other's little fingers, and all the other clichés that fit, she thought with a chuckle.

"Of course you can go," her boss had said when she'd asked him over lunch later that same day. "You haven't taken any leave in two years. You could do with a break. In fact," Max had said, waving his fork at her, "I was going to suggest you take some holiday."

"You were not."

"Yes, I was. *Strongly* suggest, in fact," he'd said in between mouthfuls. "How long do you want?"

"Just two weeks, I think. That'll be enough."

"Take three."

"No, no. I don't want to be away for so long. I have cases . . ."

"We'll meet tomorrow to review your case list and I'll split them up between the rest of the team. They're quite capable of stepping in for a while."

She hadn't answered, rather concentrating on pushing her salad around on her plate.

"I'll keep tabs, Carla," he'd said. "And I'll step in if necessary. Go have some fun with your family."

"Fun," she'd muttered, more to herself than to her boss. He was being amazingly understanding about this last-minute request, but she wished he'd be less enthusiastic. Was she really so easily replaceable? As if reading her thoughts, Max tried a different angle.

"You are my most dedicated staff member, and we'll miss you—the staff, your clients—we'll all miss you. But you need a break. You've worked and studied hard for years with remarkable focus. Now you need to relax, have some fun, and forget about other people's problems for a while. We'll all be here when you get back. I doubt anything much will have changed. It's just three weeks."

She thought Max had finished his speech, but he hadn't.

"Besides, it's for family, Carla, and nothing is more important than family." He'd taken the last piece of soft, white baguette and mopped up the remaining sauce on his plate. "Friends and colleagues come and go, but family, they're God's gift to us. You have a loving family who care about you, who want to see you, and you know very well that's not something to be taken for granted. So, you're going to go and see them and recharge your batteries at the same time. That's an order. You'll thank me for it when you come back, all bright-eyed and bushy-tailed. And you'll be a better counsellor for it."

Carla's first degree had been in nursing, specializing in midwifery. Even before she'd finished, top of her class, she'd decided she wanted to work with the less privileged communities in and around the Cape area. So she'd signed up for a second degree in social work, at which she'd also excelled.

Conscious of the lengthy path she was taking toward financial independence, Carla had done her best to help pay her board and tuition by waitressing and doing other odd jobs throughout most of her studies. It had been a tough few years, but she'd managed. Following graduation, she'd completed her apprenticeship at the Bay Church Youth Center under the guidance of its very likeable and visionary leader, Pastor Max Spencer.

Remaining at the youth center as a full-time social worker was the obvious choice and Carla had quickly become a valuable member of Max's team, respected and loved by the people with and for whom she worked. But she was a perfectionist and a workaholic and hadn't yet developed the art of setting boundaries or created much of a life for herself outside of work. Apart from daily runs along the beach promenade and church on Sundays, the Center *was* her life.

Not that she lacked opportunities. There was a long line of potential and hopeful suitors, each of whom she had gently but firmly turned down. She'd tried dating in the past but had never found anyone interesting enough to warrant taking it beyond an awkward first dinner. Lately, she'd simply preferred to refuse the many invitations and throw all her energy into her work.

In any case, although she hadn't admitted it to anyone, her heart already belonged to someone else. Sadly, she was sure *that* particular relationship—if it could be called that—was an impossible dream she'd eventually have to put behind her. Her life was here, in Cape Town. There were people here who depended on her. She couldn't just up and leave on a whim, a fantasy.

But all the same, it would be good to see him . . .

"Perhaps you're right," Carla had said. "But three weeks, Max? What on earth am I going to do there for three whole weeks? I'll go stir crazy."

"No, you won't. Read books, eat, sleep, watch bad TV movies, or even good ones. You'll no doubt run hundreds of kilometers and even find some people to look after, but please, just make sure you relax. Try to enjoy yourself, Carla. You're going on holiday, for goodness sake, not pulling teeth."

Carla had laid her fork down and folded her arms on the table in front of her. "You win, I'll go. But if I get bored or my sister drives me crazy, I'm coming back early."

"I thought you liked your sister. Why would she drive you crazy?"

"I do, at least one of them. But there's two." Carla shook her head dismissively. "It's a long story . . ." And she had no intention of telling it. Instead, she'd signaled to the waitress to bring their bill.

That had been two weeks ago and now here she was, with only a couple of days left before her first visit home in just over two years. She was actually beginning to look forward to it. It would be wonderful to see her parents, and Becky, Joe, and her nephews. And Jake.

She wished she didn't feel so apprehensive about seeing Lori again. To say she was unenthusiastic about the upcoming reunion would be a massive understatement. She determined she'd have to make an effort.

"For Mum and Dad's sake," she said to herself out loud as she parked, switched off the ignition, and climbed out of the old car. "It'll be fun," she tried to convince herself. "It'll be fine."

Nope. It probably wouldn't. But there was nothing she could do about it. She'd just have to suck it up.

"Whatever," she muttered to herself as she pulled the stairwell door open and headed for the center's main meeting room. She pushed the gnawing anxiety deeper down into her gut as she entered the room and took her place at the table. Right now, she had work to do, and nothing else was as important.

Carla bought a frothy coffee in a large paper cup and made her way from the kiosk to a table by the window overlooking the runway. She'd caught an early morning flight out of Cape Town, and was waiting for her next flight in the departure lounge of Johannesburg's Oliver Tambo airport. She'd completed the shopping she hadn't had time for in Cape Town, so she could now sit down and relax.

Sipping her coffee, she watched a massive international plane being directed into its parking bay.

"Hello Carla."

She started at the sound of her name and then slowly and deliberately put her coffee cup down on the slightly sticky table before turning to look up.

"Hello Lori," she answered with a calm she didn't feel, as if she'd seen her yesterday. She didn't bother to get up. "Dad told me you'd be catching this flight."

"Saves him an extra trip to town if we both arrive at the same time. Makes sense," Lori said, parking her trolley case next to the chair opposite Carla. "May I join you?"

"Ja, of course. I thought Noya and Jonathan would be coming with you."

"Yes, they really wanted to, but they couldn't in the end. I'm hoping they'll come for the last week, but I'm not sure. Prior commitments."

Carla continued to drink her coffee and stare out the window at the suitcases rolling out of the huge, parked plane onto a conveyor belt to be picked up at the bottom and chucked unceremoniously onto a waiting trolley.

"How are you?" Lori asked after a few moments' silence.

"Um, I'm fine, thanks."

Their flight was announced and Carla stood up quickly, relieved to end the uneasy encounter. "That's us," she said, gathering her things.

They queued, boarded, and found their seats—several rows apart, Carla noted with relief. Buckled in, she watched the security film and then stared out the small, oval window at the vanishing airport buildings as the plane taxied, gained speed, and took off.

It was official: this was going to be horrible.

Lori felt exhausted by it all: the last hectic days, the long night flight from Israel, and now the tension of her first meeting with Carla that had been as bad as she'd anticipated. Her efforts to be civil had been met with icy indifference. Perhaps she shouldn't have come after all but there was nothing she could do about it now.

She squeezed her eyes tight shut against the irritation and was soon sound asleep, waking up with a start as the stewardess announced preparations for landing. A little while later, the plane was on the ground and trundling towards a small collection of one-story buildings.

Ndola Airport. Lori smiled. It didn't look as though it had changed a bit since the days she had flown to and from boarding school in South Africa. She gripped the railing while stepping cautiously down the narrow metal stairway, then followed the other passengers across the tarmac and into a low building with a curved roof of green corrugated iron.

Once inside, she joined the end of the queue in front of the customs desk labeled *Visitors* and waited patiently for her passport check. Although Lori had been born in Zambia, she now held visitor status only with no rights beyond that.

The passengers' suitcases had been brought from the plane by tractor and trailer and were now being passed through a hole in the wall behind the customs desks. Several shabbily uniformed men set them in rows, ready for collection by their respective owners. Standing on tip-toe, Lori sighed with relief when she spotted her suitcase but it was another half hour before her passport was inspected and stamped with great deliberation.

Once past the painfully slow customs process, she accepted the help of a porter who loaded her case onto a trolley with only three working wheels and pushed it toward the exit. She'd have to tip him, but she didn't mind. Where was Paddy? Carla was nowhere to be seen either; perhaps they'd already gone out to the car, she thought.

Suddenly, she saw the handsome man standing by the exit, head and shoulders taller than everyone around him. Untidy blond curls framed a strong, suntanned face which broke into a wide grin as he spotted her. Lori dodged past the porter and ran the rest of the way, laughing as he caught her up in a bear-hug.

"Hello Titch," he said in a deep voice that entirely suited his impressive size.

"Jake," she said, a small catch in her voice. "How wonderful to see you. Did Dad send you here to fetch us? You poor thing. Have you been waiting long? Where's Carla?"

"Out by the car already, and yes, I'm doing the honors for your Dad." Jake tipped the porter, took charge of the luggage trolley and led the way across the parking lot.

"Oh, there she is." Lori noticed Carla standing by Jake's dusty jeep and looked at her properly for the first time. Tall and slim with wavy, dark-red hair cascading over one shoulder, 29-year-old Carla carried herself with an elegance that made even her traveling outfit of jeans, white T-shirt, and sneakers look like a million dollars. Stylish sunglasses hid her astonishing Maguire eyes but not her flawless, creamy skin, sculpted cheekbones and full, sensuous lips. Wherever she went, Carla turned heads, but she was either unaware or uninterested in the effect she had on others.

"Goodness, she really is beautiful, isn't she?" Lori admitted almost grudgingly.

"Yeah, she certainly is," Jake said. "When did you last see her?"

"We've been rather good at avoiding each other for the last ten years."

"Well, it's about time you both stopped that nonsense," Jake said.

"We're here now, aren't we?" Lori said, a little snappishly.

"Try to play nice, Titch." Jake grinned down at her. "Your mother's counting on it."

Carla climbed into the back seat as Jake packed Lori's luggage into the back of the large four-by-four vehicle. Lori settled into the front passenger seat and they were soon weaving their way out of the airport parking lot and onto the main road southwards.

Lori and Jake had a lot of catching up to do since they'd last seen each other and made the most of the two-and-a-half-hour drive. While they chatted, Lori kept an eye on the passing road-side scenes. Make-shift wooden tables piled with pyramids of bright red tomatoes and beige sweet potatoes stood alongside tall hessian sacks bulging with home-made charcoal, their sellers waving for attention.

They turned off the main road and drove deeper into the rural area. Jake occasionally tried to include Carla in the conversation but received only monosyllabic answers in return. Lori chattered on as she watched barefoot children run out of mud-walled houses to shout and wave at the passing car. High wire fences around large fields planted with crops indicated they were coming closer to the farming area where Lori had grown up.

When at last Jake steered the jeep off the tarmac onto a wide dirt road, Lori fell silent. After another couple of kilometers, he turned onto a single-track road of deep red earth that led straight down toward the heart of Kalulu Ranch.

Under the dark-green canopy of evergreens they drove, and over the hump-back stone bridge spanning a clear-running stream. Lori opened her mouth to tell Jake about her dream but quickly shut it again. It was too soon, and besides, she didn't want to talk about it with Carla in the car. The memory of Tom it so vividly represented belonged to her and Jake, no-one else.

And so, Lori said nothing as they traveled on down the long red road, through a large pillared gate and on towards the house. As they scrunched to a stop on the driveway, Jake gave her hand a reassuring squeeze. She smiled up at him as she wiped her cheeks dry with her free hand and then turned to meet their welcoming party.

Albeit bittersweet, as always, it was wonderful to be back home.

Part Two

"Our siblings push buttons that cast us in roles we felt sure we had let go of long ago—the baby, the peacekeeper, the caretaker, the avoider ... It doesn't seem to matter how much time has elapsed or how far we've traveled."

Jane Mersky Leder

Chapter 4

Lori surfaced slowly, as if from watery depths, to the distant and gentle sound of harmonious singing. She stretched, relishing the cool of the sheets on the unslept-in side of the double bed.

Traditions were good, and the morning prayer song led by Paddy's foreman before the workers started their day's tasks was one of her favorites. The sweet melody of a hymn sung *a cappella*, Africa-style, had to be one of the most beautiful sounds in the world, she thought; it never failed to move her deeply.

The singing was replaced by the noise of first one tractor and then another starting up. The day's farm activities had begun.

Usually, Lori would jump up the minute she was fully awake. But this first morning, she lay still and looked around the room through the veil of mosquito netting suspended and draped over the four-poster bed.

This was the room she'd grown up in. Large with a high, beamed ceiling and a huge window looking out over the back garden, fruit trees and fields beyond, its décor had metamorphosed through the years, as she had. So much had happened; how much *she'd* changed. She was a very different person now from the carefree twin sister she'd been before the accident; and different again from the angry, rebellious teenager whose world had been turned upside down by an unbearable loss.

She allowed her mind to run back—up to a point, not too far back—a rare occurrence. She'd been an unhappily wild teenager, closed to anything good and consumed with guilt if she ever laughed or felt the least bit happy. Burning up inside, she'd done everything she could to disappoint and hurt those around her. Even though she'd known it wasn't their fault, she couldn't seem to help herself.

As soon as she'd finished boarding school in South Africa, she'd bought herself a ticket to Israel with all the pocket-money she'd saved, on the basis of a whim and someone else's stories of the 'kibbutz experience' there. She wanted to get as far away as possible from everything and everyone, and Israel had seemed a good place to start. She'd ended up on a kibbutz near the sea, somewhere south of the coastal city of Haifa.

Lori had embraced the Israeli way of life in all its raw informality. She'd thrived in an environment where no-one knew her or expected anything of her; no-one pitied her or watched what they said around her. It was a country where grief and loss were sadly very much a part of life; she wasn't the only one who'd tragically lost a brother. She'd felt alive and free and had fallen in love with the controversial land and its multi-faceted people.

When her year's stint as a kibbutz volunteer was done, she found a job on the next-door *moshav* where she soon caught the eye of a land-owner's son, Yoni. When her visa ran out and she had to leave the country, she and Yoni caught a ferry to Greece. Her plan had been to see some of the islands and then return home to Africa to recoup funds and plan her next trip.

But Yoni hadn't wanted to let her go. "Marry me," he'd said one day as they sat on a Greek-island beach of bright white stones. In a moment of madness—or perhaps it was the sudden thrill of the effect this would be sure to have on her family—she'd said yes. The very next day, wearing a white cotton dress she'd bought in the market and a hand-made wreath of wild flowers in her hair, she'd become Mrs. Yoni Barkan.

She was barely 20 years old.

To say those first few years hadn't been easy was a massive understatement. Forty-year old Lori cringed and shied away from thinking about them too deeply. Few newlyweds found marriage easy to adjust to, but throwing differences of language, culture, and religion into the mix intensified the challenge a hundred-fold. To make it worse, not everyone who'd been so friendly to her when she was just a visitor or passer-by showed the same understanding and acceptance now that she was someone who'd married one of their own most eligible bachelors.

Jonathan was born not long after her 22nd birthday, and Lori found that motherhood filled at least part of the gaping emptiness within her. Her baby girl, Noya, was born during her 24th year, and she'd felt happy with her pigeon pair. She'd realized by then that her relationship with Yoni would never be built on the same kind of passionate adoration her parents shared. Once she'd recognized that fact, she found she was able to make the choice to come to terms with it. Yoni was a wonderful father and a good, kind, and faithful husband and provider; she had no reason to complain. And so, they created a home and a life together and were content.

Once she'd conquered the Hebrew language with its alphabet that was no more than hieroglyphics to her at the outset, she studied to be an English teacher and then a sports teacher and landed a job in the local senior school. She was surprised to discover that she loved teaching. And besides, the work gave her a daily timetable that suited her own children as they grew up and went to school. She'd never regretted that decision.

As the years passed, Lori gained maturity and perspective, and with that came reconciliation and improved relations with her parents. She found that as soon as she made the first step toward change, they were there, ready and waiting, full of love and forgiveness. The Bible story of the prodigal son and his father had always made her cry.

The Lori who'd come back to Kalulu for her first visit home as a young wife and mother was a very different person compared to the angry 19-year-old who'd walked out little more than three years earlier. She'd been back many times during the eighteen years since then, as often as money had allowed. Yoni had only accompanied her a few times, but she'd always brought the children. This was her first solo visit she realized as she kicked off the covers and emerged from under the mosquito net.

She pulled on her robe as she crossed the room to look at the enlarged photograph in its wooden frame that stood on the chest of drawers. She picked it up and stared down at the three laughing children's faces: Jake's, Tom's and hers. As always, it transported her back in time to that family camping trip with the Hamiltons, the Maguires' close friends and neighbors. Their last holiday with Tom.

Paddy's photograph captured the essence of that happy time and of his 14-year-old twins' relationship—with each other and with their best friend, Jake. Sun-kissed and wet from swimming, arms around each-other's shoulders, the three were laughing into the camera, a perfect picture of carefree youth and camaraderie.

She and Tom had been as close to identical as fraternal twins could possibly be: same smile, same large, darkly lashed green-blue eyes (the 'Maguire eyes' as everyone who knew the family called them), same jet-black hair and smooth, sun-browned, slightly freckled skin. Lori caressed the image of her brother's face before setting the photograph down again next to the vase of her mother's roses.

"Want some tea?"

Startled, Lori whirled around to see Paddy standing by the door. Of course; having set the day's farm work in motion, Paddy always came back to the house for morning tea with Beth. She didn't know how long he'd been standing there, watching her in silence. She just knew that she couldn't bear the pain in his eyes. She nodded and gulped against the sudden lump in her throat, not trusting herself to speak.

"Come," he said holding his hand out to her. "Come join us."

Beth was reading, perched up in bed against a small mountain of pillows, a soft, baby-blue shawl around her shoulders.

"Hello darling," she said as she took her reading glasses off the end of her nose and laid her Bible aside. "Come to join us for tea?"

Lori slid under the blankets next to her and gave her a hug.

"If you don't mind, Mama. No sugar thanks, Dad."

Lori loved this large bed with its wooden headboard displaying intricate carvings of Zambian village scenes: tiny grass-roofed huts; menfolk sitting around wood fires topped with smoking pots; traditionally-dressed women with large bowls of pineapples or stacks of firewood balanced on their heads; children at play; chickens, dogs and even a couple of goats in a grassy corner.

The headboard was the loving and painstaking work of Benson, the extraordinarily talented carpenter who had appeared on the farm one day, long ago, his few belongings tied onto the back of a rickety old bicycle. He had heard about a new boss, a good boss, on this farm, he'd explained to young Paddy, and thought that maybe this new, good boss would give him work and a place to live.

"What can you do?" Paddy had asked.

"I can make very nice things for your house from wood," Benson said, gesturing toward the roofless walls of the main house that was still a work in progress. "Tables and chairs and things," he had added hopefully.

Paddy had trusted his instincts and given the poor man a chance—and he wasn't disappointed. With no formal training but the gifted hands of a natural-born artist, Benson truly loved working with wood. He created many of the beautiful wooden furnishings that graced the Maguire family home, including the four-poster bed. But it was his dry sense of humor and generous spirit that had made him one of the Maguire family's most beloved and valued employees for the rest of his life.

Now, early on this April morning, Lori watched Paddy as he poured milk and tea into three of the four china cups laid out on the tray. He handed two to Beth and Lori, and gently shifted the reluctant Staffordshire bull terrier off the armchair.

"Come on, old girl," he said to the disgruntled dog. "You really are taking more and more liberties these days."

"She's entitled," Beth said with mock indignation. "Come here, Toffee, darling." She set her tea-cup down on her bedside table. "I'll give you all the cuddles you want."

"I see you've replaced us all no problem, Mum," Lori said.

"You're the one who chose to live so far away," Beth said, laughing.

"Ouch."

"What's so funny?" Carla stood at the door, her running gear and slightly flushed face indicating she'd already done her kilometers for the day.

"Want some tea?" Paddy asked, already pouring another cup.

"Come join us, darling," Beth said. "There's plenty of room."

"Yes, thanks, I'll have a quick cup, Dad, but I'm all sweaty so I'll just sit here." Carla perched on the end of the bed at Beth's feet and sipped her tea.

"You should have woken me, Carla. I could've done with a run," Lori said, feeling a bit guilty about her lazy morning.

"I prefer to run alone," Carla said coolly. "I like to keep my own pace."

"Fair enough, but sometimes it's fun to run with someone else, for a challenge or just for the company. You should try it sometime; you might even enjoy it." Lori was aware she sounded waspish but she'd tried to be civil, to reach out and breach the gap. Why couldn't Carla make an effort as well?

Carla set her empty cup down on the tray and stood up. "Thanks for the tea, Dad. I'm going to shower. When's breakfast?" she asked as she headed out the door.

"Eight, as usual, dear," Beth called after her. "Plenty of time."

Irritated by the exchange and Carla's attitude, Lori set her cup down on the bedside table and climbed out of the oversized bed.

"Why does she have to be so . . . so . . . stuck up?" she hissed.

"Come on Lori," Paddy said. "If you girls have issues, then you've got to work them out. Don't ruin this family time, please."

"Yes, we do have issues, Dad," Lori shot back. "I must admit I don't remember why, specifically; we just do. I guess we simply don't like each other." Lori paused at the door to look back at her father. "I will do *my* best not to ruin the holiday, Dad, I promise. But just remember, it takes two." She hesitated then added, "Thanks for the tea. I'm going to get dressed for breakfast."

Paddy covered his face with his hands, feeling tired as if it was the end of the day rather than only the beginning. He hated discord. Elbows on his bare knees, he ran his hands through his still-thick hair, delaying the moment when he'd have to look at his wife who would, no doubt, be close to tears.

"Well," he said as he eventually raised his eyes to face her. "This has come boiling to the surface even quicker than we expected."

He sighed and then frowned as he looked at Beth. Eyes narrowed and mouth set, she was not wearing the tearful expression he'd anticipated.

"I'm not surprised in the least," Beth said as she pushed her feet into their waiting slippers and pulled on her robe. "It's going to take a whole lot of prayer and patience on our part, but they'll come right. Mae arrives today and she'll help. This time together will be good, Paddy, you'll see."

"I hope you're right," Paddy muttered as she disappeared into their bathroom. He wasn't feeling nearly so confident.

Chapter 5

The dining room was full of warm morning sunshine, but breakfast was a chilly affair. Beth's stoic efforts to lift the mood had fallen flat and she was visibly relieved when Becky's head popped around the door.

"Am I too late for coffee?"

"Becky, sweetheart. Come in, come in. I'll go fetch you a mug."

"Don't worry, I'll get it," Becky said, but Beth hurried into the kitchen behind her.

"Oh, darling, it's awful," Beth whispered. "You can cut the air with a knife in there. Dad's just shut down, eating his porridge in silence. You know how he hates conflict . . ."

"Mum, you're sounding manic. What on earth is going on?"

"I've tried, darling, I really have. I know it'll be fine, but . . ." Beth picked out Becky's favorite coffee mug from the cupboard. "I'm just so glad you're here now. Please stay, for as long as you can, at least until Aunt Mae gets here."

"Oh, Mum, it can't be as bad as all that."

"It is, and worse." Beth stared at her daughter with wild eyes until she noticed the expression on Becky's face and they both dissolved into muffled giggles.

"Well, I'll be off then," Paddy said with a look of blatant relief as Beth and Becky came back into the dining room, taking his hat off its hook by the door. "I'll be back with Aunt Mae before tea-time, traffic willing."

"Want company, Dad?"

"No, no, don't bother, Carla," Paddy said quickly. "Thanks anyway. I've got some business to do and spare parts to buy in town before your Aunt's plane lands at two. You just relax and enjoy being at home. You can keep an eye on Rex for me."

Settling his hat on his head, Paddy kissed his wife on the cheek.

"Good luck," he whispered in her ear before disappearing out the door with a cheery "Bye, girls. Have fun."

Beth watched him go with a feeling of envy and then bracing her shoulders and pulling the corners of her mouth into a bright smile, she turned back to face her three daughters. "Coffee?"

Carrying a vase of freshly cut roses for the lounge, Beth stopped in the archway to absorb the rare scene before her, storing it up in that special mother-memory space. She felt a rush of gratitude as she watched Becky chatting with her sisters; her arrival had palpably lightened the mood of the morning. In fact, Beth thought, Becky's sweet, kind nature had always had an oil-on-water calming effect on her more fiery-spirited siblings.

The sisters were working their way through the stack of family photo albums that Beth had carefully created over the years. They looked happy and at ease as they reminisced and laughed. Maybe things weren't so bad after all, Beth thought; perhaps she and Paddy had been imagining or exaggerating things. All sisters bicker every now and then . . .

"Oh, my goodness," Lori said, laughing. "Joe looks the most uncomfortable groom, like he's wearing sackcloth or something."

"He was uncomfortable," Becky said. "If he'd had his way, he'd have worn his work shorts and boots down the aisle."

"You were totally gorgeous. That dress was so perfect for you, and you look so happy. Makes me want to cry all over again."

"Ah, did you cry at my wedding, Lor?"

"Of course I did. Only more discreetly than Daddy, otherwise I would have botched the make-up you made me wear."

"Look at what a stunning bride Mummy was," Carla exclaimed with genuine pride. "Look at her." She held out a photo that had come loose from one of the older albums to Becky.

Beth set the roses down on the coffee table and leaned over Becky's shoulder to look at the slightly faded photograph.

"You're so young and beautiful, Mum, and Daddy was really good looking, wasn't he?" Becky said.

"The catch of the province," Beth said, taking the photo to look at it more closely. "I was over the moon that day. Couldn't believe he was mine," she said dreamily. "But I'm afraid there were a *lot* of broken hearts. All the other hopeful ladies . . ."

"Oh Mum, no-one else ever stood a chance. Daddy only ever had eyes for you. He's told me that himself," Lori said. "And you still gaze at each other sometimes like newly-weds."

"Romance takes work, make no mistake about it," Beth said as she joined Becky on the couch. "We had our hard times, but we never broke our golden rule."

"Never go to bed angry," Lori and Becky chimed in unison, then laughed.

"Never underestimate the power of that simple rule," Beth said, frowning.

"It's a good rule, Mum. Really good rule."

"You can mock, Lori."

"I'm not, Mum, I promise. You ask Yoni; it's our golden rule too, or at least we try."

"Anyway," Beth said, changing the subject. "How did you all get into the photo albums? You're meant to be planning my party."

"That's what we started off doing," Becky said, "and then we were thinking about doing a bit of a presentation, a 'This is Your Life' kind of thing, which led us to the photo albums."

"Oh, *please* don't do all that," Beth said. "Isn't it meant to be a garden party? Let's talk about the *food*—far more important."

"What I don't understand, Mum," Carla said, still paging through her parent's wedding photographs, "is how you could have left England and Auntie Mae to come out to Africa with Dad. You didn't have a clue about what you were getting yourself into, did you? And you and Auntie Mae were almost joined at the hip you were so close, weren't you? Didn't it just break your heart?"

Beth was silent for a minute. "It did break my heart," she said softly, "but I loved your Dad, and this is where he wanted to be. He belonged in Africa, I knew that. This farm was his dream, and I loved him enough to support him in it, even though it was hard at first."

"But what about *your* dream?" Carla asked.

"Daddy *was* my dream," Beth said simply. "You kids, our family, our beautiful home, our life together, the food we produce, the people we serve—that was all my dream too."

"Hmmm," Carla said as she closed and put the old album aside; she didn't appear to be convinced.

"That's what you do, Carla, when you fall in love with someone," Lori said. "You hook your futures up to the same star, even if it takes you across continents and away from family."

"Don't patronize me, Lori," Carla said sharply. "I just don't think it's fair one person has to give up everything familiar and dear and important in her life to follow after someone else's dream. *I* wouldn't do it."

"Really? Are you sure about that?" Becky asked.

"It's not about giving *up* everything, darling," Beth said. "It's about creating a new life together, with the person you love and who you've chosen to spend the rest of your life with. It's a good thing."

"I did it," Lori said matter-of-factly. "And survived. Eventually . . ."

"Well, *you* did it on purpose," Carla said quietly as she closely examined a photograph.

"Excuse me? What did you say?" Lori's tone was sharp.

Carla looked up at Lori, her eyes narrowed and cold. "I said, you did it on purpose. You wanted to get as far away as you could without a second thought for your parents or anyone else, for that matter."

"What absolute rubbish. Where on earth did you come up with that?"

"How else do you explain what you did? *And* where you landed up—in Israel of all places," Carla said with a sarcastic smirk.

"I'd rather you didn't talk about something you know absolutely nothing about. You've no idea . . ." Lori's voice was low and trembling with anger and hurt.

Beth pressed her fingers to her temples; she felt a headache coming on. She looked pleadingly at Becky, silently willing her to steer the conversation away from the dangerously muddy waters it was plunging into.

"So, are we going to make this a sit-down thing with tables set out in the garden or a cocktail-buffet mingly kind of party?" Becky asked quickly with artificial brightness. "What do you prefer, Mum?"

Beth threw a look of gratitude at Becky. "You girls can do whatever you want," she said with a dismissive wave. "I'm trying to think what to do for tea this afternoon."

Becky threw a cushion at each of her sisters who looked up at her in surprise. "Come on guys," Becky said. "Don't do this. Be nice, okay?"

Carla stood up and kissed Becky on the top of her head as she passed behind the couch. "I think a sit-down garden dinner will be fun, but you decide," she said, heading out towards the kitchen. "Don't worry about tea, Mum. I'll make a cake for Auntie Mae."

"Lor?"

"What?" Lori stood up and stretched leisurely as if the last few minutes had never happened. "Oh, the party. What did you call it? A 'cocktail-buffet mingly thing'? That sounds like fun," she said, going out onto the verandah.

"Perfect," Becky moaned, covering her face with a cushion. "Just perfect."

"I told you," Beth said. Becky reappeared from behind the cushion and Beth gave her a wry smile. "But thanks for trying, darling, all the same."

Chapter 6

Beth settled herself on the couch after lunch. Becky was having a rest in her room, and besides, she didn't want to risk missing Paddy and Mae's arrival. She made herself comfortable against the cushions and found her place in the book she was reading. But she soon laid it down, unable to concentrate.

She was excited about Mae's impending arrival—Paddy had called to say she'd landed safely and they were on their way home—and the earlier talk about her wedding and leaving England had sparked some memories. She didn't allow herself the luxury of reflection very often but now her mind strayed back to those early days.

She had been a mere 10 years old and Mae 13 when their warm and happy home was shattered by the untimely death of their parents in a car crash. Their beautiful English country home had been sold, and the confused and broken-hearted little girls were taken to live with their mother's elder sister in her austere London apartment. Their aunt had never approved (or perhaps she'd been jealous) of what she'd called her sister's 'frivolous character' and loving marriage. The girls had no choice but to try and rebuild their lives in the foreign atmosphere, the unhappy home making them cling together as each other's sole source of comfort and strength.

As soon as it could be arranged, their aunt had sent them off to boarding school (another rude shock), which made Mae even more fiercely protective of Beth. As soon as they were legally old enough and able to support themselves, they had moved out of their aunt's home. Mae found a job as a secretary; it wasn't her dream but earned her a living and helped to support Beth's studies in nursing school. In a turn of events that would have amused their mother, the feisty Mae soon caught the eye of a wealthy businessman whom she quickly married.

John Lavender had been thirteen years older than Mae, but she loved him for his quiet dependability. In return, he had adored his vivacious young wife and was eager to give her anything to ensure her happiness. They had moved into an elegant London townhouse and acquired a country cottage for weekend breaks. At last, Mae had been able to fulfil her dream of attending university where she'd excelled, going on to become a member of faculty and one of her students' favorite lecturing professors.

Mae had made one condition when John asked her to marry him: that their home would be Beth's home, for as long as she needed. John was no fool and agreed without hesitation. Beth, on the other hand, had taken some persuading but eventually agreed to move in with them after their wedding; she was away at college most of the time anyway.

It had been a good arrangement and worked well, mostly due to John's placid and accepting character and Beth's sensitivity. But when, after her graduation, an opportunity arose to join a group of medical volunteers on a six-month mission to a remote corner of Africa, Beth had jumped at the chance. It was there she'd met Paddy.

Beth remembered how, as a young and impressionable English rose, she'd been swept off her feet by the ruggedly handsome young man. Her feelings and the impossibility of the situation had so terrified her that she'd fled back home as soon as the six months were finished. The intrepid Paddy had refused to admit defeat and followed her over to England, determined to win her over.

She smiled to herself, remembering the tale of his brave yet awkward venture into the velvety realm of a fancy London jewelers where he'd bought a ring he couldn't afford. With the little box hidden deep in his pocket, he'd simply appeared one day on Mae's doorstep, asking for Beth. The romantic Beth was bowled over, but Mae was not so enthusiastic.

Paddy had proposed and she'd accepted of course, but leaving Mae was one of the hardest things she'd ever had to do. But she'd done it anyway, and she and Paddy were married just months later in his mother's beautiful garden in northern Zambia.

Beth thanked God that she and Mae had managed to maintain their close and special relationship over the years, writing long and frequent letters that in the early days had sometimes taken months to receive. As time and technology progressed, keeping in touch became ever easier. All the same, Mae and John had been faithful in making annual visits to Kalulu, which had always been treasured times. This would be the third time that Mae made the journey alone.

Surely, theirs was a unique and precious sisterly relationship born out of shared tragedy and heartache, Beth pondered. No, it had also taken conscious effort and even expense on both their parts, sometimes when it couldn't be afforded. But they'd persevered, working hard to preserve their closeness in spite of living on different continents.

That's a lesson my daughters need to learn, she thought, flicking an annoying fly away from her face. But what if she and Mae had known what lay ahead for her? Would Mae have agreed to the marriage? Would Beth have let her return to England after the wedding without her?

Beth pressed her fingers to her eyes. "No regrets," she whispered, "no regrets." She really couldn't imagine a life without Paddy, whatever it had entailed. That was unthinkable.

She'd made new friends—good, close women friends—who'd helped to fill the void. Especially Sadie. Dear, sweet, eccentric Sadie Hamilton. Beth recalled her first meeting with the couple of young hippy-looking explorers who'd appeared on their doorstep all those years ago, looking for a place to camp.

They'd ended up staying at Kalulu for a month and eventually buying the farm next door, and Jake had been born not long after Beth and Paddy's own twins. They'd had so much fun together, the two families, and when tragedy struck, the Hamiltons grieved for Tom like he was their own.

It had been two years since the Hamiltons had returned to America to manage Sadie's ailing father's estate, leaving Jake to manage the farm in Zambia. Beth missed her friend terribly, but she was already well practiced at keeping long-distance relationships alive.

"*Ndona*," Jonas' deep voice broke her reverie.

"Yes?" Beth sat up quickly to look at Jonas where he stood in the arched entrance to the lounge.

"They have arrived," he announced, his beautiful white teeth lighting up his otherwise usually serious-looking face.

"Really? I didn't hear the car," Beth said, finding her shoes while trying to quickly tidy her hair. "Come, come say hello." She urged Jonas to join her as she hurried out the front door to welcome her sister.

"Hello, hello!" Even as Beth hurried towards Paddy's dusty car, her eyes turned to water.

"Hello my darling girl," Mae said as they hugged. "Don't cry, Bethy, sweetheart, don't cry."

But Beth couldn't stop the tears. The years shot away and she felt as though they were two little girls once again, a feeling no doubt heightened by her nostalgic musings and the tension of the morning.

"What a soppy bunch we are." Paddy chuckled as he wiped his eyes with the back of his hand. "Come on Jonas, let's unpack the car. I brought some boxes from town that I'll need your help with."

Tears were replaced all around by laughter, hugs and kisses as Lori, Becky and Carla joined them and joyfully embraced their aunt. Paddy took the opportunity to give Beth a loving hug.

"Are you alright, old girl?" he said as he held her tight. "Has it been horrid?"

Beth drew back to look at him. "Now and then," she said with a smile and kissed him on his cheek. "Thank you, my darling, for bringing Mae home safely."

"Tea in the garden with you and your lovely family—heaven," Mae said. She linked her arm through Beth's as they strolled towards the *lapa*.

"Coffee cake, especially for you, Auntie Mae," Carla said.

"Oh, my goodness, will you look at that? You've obviously inherited your Mother's talent for baking. And here come Jonas' delicious flapjacks. Who's going to eat all of this?"

"Don't you worry about that," Becky said. "Joe and the boys are on their way over to say hello, so the flapjacks will be gone in no time."

"Any more tea left in the pot?" Right on cue, Joe made his way over the lawn toward them, preceded by his sons.

"Mum, please can we swim now, please?" Riley pleaded.

"No, you can't. Not yet, anyway," Becky answered. "First, you'll both find your manners and say hello to Auntie Mae who's travelled all the way from England." Becky gave them a gentle shove in the direction of Mae's chair.

"Hello you gorgeous boys. Look how tall you've both grown," Mae said, amused by Ben and Riley's obedient yet slightly awkward hugs. "Go and help yourselves to a pile of those flapjacks with strawberry jam and cream—I've heard they're your favorites. Once I've finished my tea, we'll go up to the house because there are a couple of presents I think I can dig out of my suitcase that may just have your names on them," she said with a mischievous smile.

"Thank you, Auntie Mae," the boys said with wide grins.

"Hello Aunt Mae, good to see you again," Joe said, bending down to kiss her cheek. "And I heard all that," he said, grinning. "You'll spoil them rotten and then disappear back off to England, leaving us to deal with the consequences."

"Nonsense. It's my joy and duty as the great-aunt from far away," Mae said.

"I heard there's tea and cake on offer." Jake's deep voice broke through the chatter.

"Jake, come join us," Beth said. "Come say hello to Mae. Lori, please go and get Jake a cup. Don't bother with the china; he prefers the big blue mug."

"Smell the cake from your fields, did you?" Lori teased, giving him a friendly punch on the shoulder as she passed him on her way up to the house.

"No, it's my fault," Joe said. "I bumped into him in the *boma*. Told him there'd be tea and cake on offer."

"Hello Aunt Mae," Jake said, giving her an affectionate hug and kiss.

"Jake, how lovely to see you, dear. Can I cut you some of that coffee cake? It really is as delicious as it looks."

"No, no, Mae," Beth said. "Carla can do the honors, seeing as she baked it."

"Hello Carla," Jake said in a voice that made Mae sit up and take notice. She prided herself on being extremely observant of people's behavior and highly tuned to the smallest nuances that went completely over the top of most heads. She glanced around the *lapa* but sure enough, no-one else seemed to be noticing the virtual sparks that were flying between them.

Mae certainly did notice Carla's flushed cheeks as Jake joined her by the bar where she was cutting the cake, the way she ducked her head as if to hide her coy smile, and their lingering touch as Carla handed him the delicate china plate loaded with a large and indelicate slice of cake. Mae was at once amused and pleased; this would be a good match, so why were they being so bashful about it?

"Milk, no sugar, as usual?" Lori asked Jake cheerily as she re-appeared, mug in hand.

At the sound of Lori's voice, Carla pulled her hand away from Jake as if she'd been burned. Turning away abruptly, she hurried over to sit next to Beth.

"Oh dear," Mae muttered under her breath as it all became a little clearer. It would seem that Lori was unaware of the budding romance and that Carla wanted to keep it that way. Well, that's just silly, thought Aunt Mae. I wonder if Beth . . .

"How was your trip, Aunt Mae?" Jake interrupted her musings with his polite enquiry. Sitting opposite her in the two-seater vacated by Carla he was focusing all his attention on her, rather deliberately Mae thought, but she'd play along.

"Oh, long and boring as usual," Mae said, "and I should be totally exhausted. But I managed to sleep on the plane and somehow, this place always totally energizes me. So much going on."

If Jake understood her insinuation, he ignored it.

"Maybe it's our good, clean air," he said, "rather than your London smog."

"I don't live in London anymore, dear," Mae said. "When my dear John passed away a few years ago, I moved into what was once our weekend cottage in a very lovely little village near Oxford. It's what we call 'out in the country'."

"It's gorgeous there, a real calendar-picture type of village. You'd love it, Jake," Lori said, sitting cross-legged on the couch next to her friend. "Mind you, you probably wouldn't fit through the front door. All so low-ceilinged, those cottages, as if they were built for little people."

"I think they were," Mae said. "The older ones, anyway. People used to be smaller, didn't they? In England, anyway."

"Not the same thing," Jake said, a large portion of cake poised on the tiny silver fork. "Can't compare your country air, probably tainted by smoke from some factory or massive city just half an hour away, to ours out here in the African bush."

"Don't mind him, Aunt Mae. He's just being argumentative for the sake of it," Lori said.

Jake grinned. "I'm only teasing. I'd love to see your country village someday, Aunt Mae. I remember Aunt Beth's photographs from her last visit."

"You're very welcome, any time," Mae said, and then added nonchalantly: "Perhaps you could come over with Carla one day. She's never been to visit me either."

Laughing, Lori turned towards Jake. "That'll be the day . . ."

But Jake was silent, his head down as if concentrating on the remains of his cake, his cheeks slightly flushed. Lori stared at him, her mouth open, her eyes widening as if in disbelief and then narrowing. After an awkward pause, she stood up.

"You've got to be kidding me," she snarled. Mae wondered if she even realized she'd said it aloud.

"What's that, dear?" Beth asked. She glanced at Mae with a slightly confused look on her face, but Mae just gave her what she hoped was a reassuring smile. The cat was out the bag and well and truly amongst the pigeons, it would seem, whether Carla liked it or not.

"Um, um . . ." Lori pressed her fingers to her eyes and shook her head as if to dislodge what she'd just seen. Her cheeks were flushed an angry red and Mae wondered if she was going to punch her friend or burst into tears. No doubt to avoid doing either she left the *lapa*, muttering "I can't be here," as she went.

"What? Why ever not?" Beth asked.

"I . . . I need to call Yoni and the kids," she said as she strode towards the house, balled fists at her sides.

Mae realized with stark clarity what she'd only vaguely felt a few minutes ago: this wasn't just a new and exciting match between two lovely single and probably very well-suited young people. The proverbial boat that was being rocked was already exceedingly fragile, even volatile. She noticed Beth was looking even more confused and concerned and immediately regretted her earlier frivolous remark. She had obviously poked a bear.

She glanced around the *lapa* to see how far the ripple of tension had spread. The menfolk seemed oblivious and Joe was chatting to Paddy about a new tractor he was considering buying, Jake now turning to join their conversation.

"More tea for anyone?" Beth asked, as though trying to restore the mood.

Becky hauled herself out of her chair and without a word walked up to the house. Only Carla sat motionless, Mae noticed, her face like a beautiful, expressionless mask.

Becky found Lori pacing the grassy quad around which the Spanish-style farmhouse had been built. Over a century ago, some homes in the African bush were built in this way to keep young children safe from the likes of lions and hyenas. Paddy and Beth had maintained the design, not from necessity but just because they liked the idea of a secluded inner garden.

"Hmmm, thought you were making a phone call," Becky said, lowering herself onto a wooden bench standing among pots of flowers.

Lori scowled at her but didn't answer.

"Come on Lor," Becky said, patting the empty space beside her. "Come sit down and talk to me."

"You can't fix this, Becks. Don't think you're going to just smooth this one away."

"Will you please just come and sit down? You're making me dizzy." Becky patted the bench again. "Please Lor, come tell me what's freaked you out so badly."

"You know perfectly well what's freaked me out. Don't pretend, Becks. That's just annoying." Lori sat down next to Becky and covered her face with her hands. "Jake and *Carla* . . . really?"

"Alright, alright, so there may be something going on between them. So what?"

"So what?" Lori said, dropping her hands from her face and staring wide-eyed at her younger sister. "*Seriously?*"

"Yes, so what?" Becky said calmly. She reached out and took Lori's brown-skinned hand in her own paler one. Their differing skin tones had always amused her. The twins had inherited their father's dark Irish looks, and she their mother's English-rose complexion, while Carla was an exotic blend of both. She pulled her thoughts back to the crisis at hand.

"I know he's your best friend, Lor," Becky said, feeling like she was standing on the edge of a cliff, "but you're married and living a million miles away. You have Yoni and Jonathan and Noya, and your whole busy life in a place where *you* chose to make your home. Jake goes home to an empty house at the end of every day. Don't you want him to have what we have? *I* do." She paused. "And beyond that, you know he's always adored Carla."

"Not like this!" Lori was fighting back tears. "She's ten years younger than him, for goodness' sake."

"So?" Becky asked. "If it doesn't matter to them, why should it bother you?"

"She'll break his heart and I'll never forgive her. Everything will be awkward and awful between Jake and Mum and Dad and . . . and all of us."

Becky was quiet for a minute and then dared to creep closer to the cliff edge. "Why are you so angry with her?" She nervously wondered if she'd gone too far, but it had to be said. "It's as if you're holding something against Carla that's just eating you up."

Lori was silent for a long time, seemingly oblivious to the tiny white butterfly flitting between her and the flowers in their pots next to the bench. Becky knew from the occasional creasing of her sister's brow into a troubled frown that she was deep in thought.

"I don't know," Lori said eventually in a low voice. "I just can't bear her." She dropped her head as though hanging it in shame. "Wow," she said, glancing up at the cloudless blue sky above them and then at her sister. "That's a terrible thing to say, isn't it?"

Becky was deeply saddened at the sight of Lori's eyes shining with tears. "Admitting there's a problem is the first step toward solving it. I've wondered about it often, why you two don't get along and what may have started it all. I remember a time when you loved

Carla to bits, when she was a baby. You and Tom were crazy about her."

"*Tom* was crazy about her."

"You both were," Becky said. "She was so beautiful and cute and funny. I felt very rejected, just so you know." She laughed. "She completely knocked me off my youngest-child-pedestal."

Lori didn't laugh with her. "I don't know, Becks. For years now, she's been totally indifferent to me. Personally, I think for the most part, she's self-absorbed and spoilt and unpleasant."

Becky frowned. "Those are hard accusations, and I don't think they're true, Lor. If that's what you think Carla's like, then you don't know her at all."

"Please don't try and paint her as an angel, Becks, because I'm not buying it."

"I'm not. We're none of us angels—far from it—but Carla's a lovely, giving, caring person."

"And I'm Mother Theresa," Lori said rolling her eyes.

"I mean it, Lor. You can't be self-absorbed and do the kind of work she does, for starters. And she's definitely not spoilt. She worked really hard to put herself through varsity, refusing almost all help from Mum and Dad just because she didn't want to be a burden to them, and wanted to make it on her own. And what else did you say? Unpleasant . . . no, she's not. She's great fun, and she's also very sweet and considerate."

Lori remained silent for a while and then almost whispered, "So, she *is* an angel."

Becky ignored the cynical remark. "She's our kid sister. She's a wonderful person and you're missing out on her. It breaks my heart, not to mention Mum and Dad's."

Silence.

Becky sighed and looked skyward as if seeking patience and guidance. Was she helping or making things worse? She really didn't know but couldn't leave it there.

"Do you know what I think, Lor?" Becky squeezed her sister's hand gently. "I think that on the surface, you and Carla are worlds apart with no hope of bridging the *abyss* that's separating you right now. It's an abyss that's grown wider and wider over the years."

Lori nodded.

"But," Becky said, "I think that right there, just under the surface, both you and Carla are dying to put all this behind you, to forgive and forget."

"Sorry Becks, but I don't agree," Lori said, pulling her hand away. "And I'll give you an example from this morning. I went to have tea with Mum and Dad, you know, in bed before breakfast. We were having a great time chatting about various things, and then Carla came in from her run. She just stood at the door, refused to join us and was totally aloof—not at all sweet or pleasant. Trying to be nice, I said it was a shame she didn't wake me as I would've come running with her. To which she answered, my dear, sweet little sister, that she preferred to run alone, thank you, and went off to shower. Charming." Lori folded her arms as if satisfied she'd proved a point.

Becky giggled. "You sound like a kid."

"I know I do. It's ridiculous," Lori said and groaned, "but I can't help it."

"I'm not buying it. The solution is there, just under the surface. You're almost best buddies."

Lori grimaced. "I highly doubt it."

"Best buddies," Becky repeated. "You'll see."

"I do love you, Sis," Lori said as she turned and hugged Becky. "*You* are the angel, the rose between us two thorns. And you're sweet to try and fix us. But don't be upset if we stay broken."

"You won't stay broken," Becky said. "I'm telling you—it's there, just beneath the surface."

"Our Becks, the everlasting optimist."

Becky stood up and stretched, pressing the palms of her hands into the small of her back. "Coming back out? I could do with another cup of tea."

"No, you go ahead," Lori said. "I'm going to call Yoni. Feel like chatting with him and the kids for a bit, if they're around, and anyway, I told Mum that's what I was doing."

Becky planted a kiss on the top of Lori's head. "Give them my love."

Chapter 7

Beth and Jonas sat at the large island in the middle of the kitchen, shelling peas and chatting amiably together.

Almost a week had passed since Mae's arrival, and this morning she'd insisted on being escorted by both Lori and Carla to watch the dipping—a weekly event that kept the cattle free from ticks and disease. While Beth appreciated Mae's tireless efforts to 'bring the girls together' as she called it, right now, she was simply enjoying the peace and quiet.

She smiled across at her old friend, Jonas. His hair was greying a bit at the temples but other than that, he was tall and strong with smooth, seemingly ageless ebony skin. Always the very embodiment of quiet courtesy and authority, he had helped her manage her household with superb efficiency for over forty years.

He'd fallen silent now, seemingly preoccupied, and Beth's thoughts wandered back to their first meeting when he'd appeared as an over-confident teenager on her doorstep, all those years ago.

"Good afternoon," he'd said when she opened the door.

He'd cycled from his home village to the young Maguire couple's new farm of virgin bush and now stood in front of her, straining to see over her shoulder into the little cottage.

"Can I help you?"

"Um, I think I will be a very good cook for you," Jonas had said, standing up very straight and looking her square in the eyes. "The very best."

"Do you know how to cook?"

"I do not cook . . . yet. But I always watch and help my mother when she cooks. It is what I like to do."

"Why don't you get a job working with cattle or driving a tractor? Wouldn't you prefer to do that?"

"No. I would like to cook. I think I will learn very quickly and become the best cook in the district."

Beth was both amused and intrigued by the thin and gangly youth with intelligent eyes.

"Do you know how to garden, or grow vegetables perhaps?"

"Ah yes. I am the one who helps my mother to grow vegetables. My father does not like me doing that and says it is work for my sisters, but I like to grow things, so I do not listen to him."

Bit of a rebel, Beth thought. "What is your name?"

"My name is Jonas," he said proudly.

"What about school? You aren't old enough to have your certificate yet."

"I do not like school." The bravado had disappeared as Jonas dropped his gaze. "The teacher says I am no good."

"How can that be? You speak very good English." Beth felt affronted for the boy. "Where did you learn to speak English?"

Jonas explained that he'd learnt from the children of the family on whose farm they'd lived when he was younger. "I taught them how to speak my language, and they taught me English. I also taught them how to play football." He puffed his chest out and grinned.

"I'll give you a job," Beth said, "on condition you finish your schooling."

Her immediate reward was a million-dollar smile. "Thank you, Mama! That is very good. But I think we can forget about the school. I do not need any certificate, especially if I am to become a very great cook."

Beth ignored his last remark. "Is this your bicycle?"

"No, this is my very big brother's bicycle. He will probably beat me for taking it."

The boy was still smiling, so Beth doubted this was true.

"I have no money to buy a bicycle of my own," he continued.

"I will loan you a bicycle, which you must look after very well. But you *will* go to school and you will come here only when you have finished your lessons. You will tell me every day what you have learned and if you have questions, I will try to help you. In return, you can help me with the vegetable garden I'm trying to make." Beth had spoken slowly and clearly to ensure he understood the terms of his employment.

"And you will learn me how to cook?"

"Yes, Jonas, I will *teach* you how to cook."

Every afternoon from then on, Jonas would ride his treasured new bicycle to Kalulu. Beth would help him with his schoolwork while he munched and slurped his way through a lunch of thickly cut sandwiches and very sweet tea.

His lessons done, they would take the path that led away from the cottage towards the stream and the site of Beth's vegetable garden. Now that she had Jonas to help her, Beth's designs for the garden had become much more ambitious, and together they'd planned and dug and planted and watered and weeded.

In addition to the wages she'd paid him, Beth had kept her promise and taught Jonas how to cook. She'd discovered he had natural talent and once something had been explained and demonstrated to him, he never forgot a recipe. Even better, he was very inventive and she encouraged him to be as creative as he dared.

Beth had quickly found herself looking forward to Jonas' arrival every day. Working hard to carve his farm out of the virgin bush and build the house of their dreams, Paddy was often out from dawn to dusk. Beth had spent hours writing almost daily letters to Mae, describing her new life in artificially glowing terms while being careful not to let her tears smudge the pages. But since Jonas' appearance, she'd felt much less lonely.

When Jonas successfully passed his school certificate, Paddy and Beth had offered to support his further education wherever he wanted, but he'd refused. He preferred to stay with them on the farm as their full-time employee. He was stubborn, and Beth had finally given up trying to persuade him otherwise.

Their initial mutual respect developed into friendship and deep loyalty—all the while within the strict bounds of respect and propriety befitting the African culture. For more than forty years, Beth and Jonas had worked, rejoiced, and mourned together. They'd both known the terrible pain of losing a child, and the shared grief in their separate darkest moments bound them closer together. They knew they could count on each other, whatever the circumstance . . .

"Hello, busy bees."

Beth was jolted back to the present by the appearance of Mae, Lori and Carla at the kitchen door, and glanced guiltily at the wall clock.

"Goodness, are you back already? You'll be grubby after being at the dip, so go and wash up and I'll make coffee. Mae, did I tell you that Jonas is about to be a grand-father again?"

"Really? What fun. Who's having a baby, Jonas?"

"Precious, my youngest daughter," he said, beaming. "I think it may be very soon."

"That's wonderful news, Jonas," Mae said, matching his smile. "I hope it'll go well for her."

The night was as still and dark as only an African bush night can be. There was no glow of reflected city lights to dilute the blackness and a solid cloud covering shrouded the otherwise brightness of countless stars and an almost-full moon. An owl hooted once, twice, behind the bedroom wing of the silent, shuttered house, and in a close-by field a solitary cow bellowed for her calf.

Beth was suddenly, instantly alert, woken by the unfamiliar sound of knocking on glass.

"*Ndona* Beth," growled a low voice, a deep-voiced man's best attempt at a whisper.

"Jonas?" Beth pulled on her robe as she emerged from beneath the mosquito net, grabbed the torch from her bedside table and flicked it on.

"Jonas," she repeated. "Is that you?"

"Yes."

"What's wrong?" She saw him now, standing on the lawn outside her window in the shaded light of his own torch held down toward the ground.

"It is Precious. Her time has come and it is not going well. She needs help." He sounded tense and upset.

Paddy had joined Beth at the window. "Don't worry, Jonas. It'll be alright," he said. "We'll come now and if necessary, we'll take Precious to the hospital. Go tell Fred to open the gate."

Without another word, Jonas vanished back into the night while Beth and Paddy quickly dressed.

"I'll wake up Carla; perhaps she can help," Paddy said as he pulled on a pair of trousers, but when they opened their bedroom door Carla was already coming up the passageway to meet them.

"What's wrong?" she asked, looking remarkably wide awake.

Beth quickly brought her up to speed. Carla ran back to her room to dress just as Lori emerged from her bedroom.

"What's happening?" she asked, sleepily.

"Precious has gone into labor and needs help," Beth said.

"Want me to do anything?"

"No thanks, darling. Carla's coming with us, but if it's complicated, we'll take Precious to the hospital in the *boma*, so we may be gone for a while. Go back to bed."

"Okay. Call if you need me," Lori mumbled as she closed her bedroom door.

Beth grabbed her medical bag, always kept at the ready for emergencies, and she and Carla crossed the quad and exited the back door to where Paddy had the car ready and waiting. They climbed in, and he sped through the now open west gate. Fred the night watchman, saluted them as they passed.

"Funny old thing," Carla said, quickly twisting her hair into a long plait.

"He insists on doing that every time he sees us," Paddy said, "although we've begged him not to. Leave-over from his army days, apparently."

"Oh dear, poor Jonas sounded so upset. I do pray it's not as serious as he made it sound." Beth wrung her hands, wanting to be there already for her friend. "Sorry to wake you, darling," she said over her shoulder to Carla, "but I'm glad you're here to help."

"I wasn't asleep yet anyway," Carla said. "Must be that dratted anti-malarial pill; gives me insomnia every time I take it. Good job it's only weekly."

"It's better than the alternative," Paddy said sternly as he took a left and drew up outside a small collection of neat brick houses. Jonas and his son-in-law were waiting impatiently outside one of two larger houses. Carla took Beth's medical bag off the back seat beside her and both women hurried into the house, leaving the men to wait outside.

A little while later, Beth emerged.

"It looks like she's going to need a C-section, Paddy, so we're going to have to take her into the hospital. Carla's getting her ready to move now. No point in us all going, so Carla and I will go in with her and Miriam."

"Wouldn't hear of it," Paddy said. "And don't try and persuade me otherwise."

Beth didn't. "Quickly, then; let's put the back seat of the car down so she can lie flat."

Jonas, Paddy and the young husband carried Precious out on a mattress, which they gently slid into the back of the car. Her mother, Miriam, climbed in beside her while Carla ran around and clambered into the other side so she could keep a close eye on the laboring young woman for the half-hour drive to the hospital.

Paddy carefully shut the rear door, sealing them in. He then asked Jonas to give him his mobile phone. Taking it, he punched in a number and handed it back. "This is the number for the hospital. Call and tell them we're coming and that Precious needs an operation. I want them to be ready for us."

Jonas nodded silently and went to stand beside Beth's passenger-seat window. He suddenly looked old with sagging shoulders, his eyes silently pleading with her to take good care of his daughter. As the car engine roared to life, Beth took both his hands in hers.

"Don't worry, old friend. Pray and have faith. She'll be alright and you'll have a new grandchild by morning," she said with an encouraging smile.

"Yes, I will pray that this will be so. Thank you, Mama," he whispered simply but with a depth of emotion that made Beth want to cry.

Chapter 8

Refreshed from an excellent night's sleep, Mae breezed into the sun-drenched dining room, ready for a hearty breakfast. Her morning cheer quickly faded as she took in the scene before her. Paddy and Beth looked weary, the lines around their shadowed eyes deeper. Lori was silently dishing out the oatmeal porridge in place of Beth, and Carla was nowhere to be seen.

"What's wrong? Has something happened?" Aunt Mae asked, feeling slightly alarmed. "Where's Carla?"

Beth smiled and shook her head. "You and your ear-plugs, Mae. I can't believe you slept through it all."

"Slept through what? What happened?"

"Jonas' daughter, Precious, had her baby last night," Beth explained. "Thank you, darling," she smiled up at Lori, taking the bowl of steaming porridge. "Very kind."

"*And?*" Mae prompted.

"Jonas woke us in the middle of the night to tell us she was in trouble. Carla and I went to try help but she needed a C-section so we took her to the hospital in the *boma*." She paused as she reached for the jug of milk. "Carla's a wonderful nurse, you know. Don't know why she gave it up."

"Oh Beth, do get on with the story. Are Precious and the baby alright?"

"Yes, of course they are. The doctor was ready and waiting for us because Jonas had phoned ahead—thanks to Paddy's clear thinking—so he had her into the operating theatre very quickly. We stayed to keep Miriam company until the operation was over."

"Who's Miriam?" Aunt Mae asked.

"Jonas' wife," Lori said, taking her seat at the table again after she'd served everyone their tea or coffee preference. "You remember her."

"Oh yes, of course," Aunt Mae said. "Lovely lady. I am useless with people's names. Such a shortcoming. And how's Precious this morning?"

"I think she's fine," Beth said. "She was rather groggy after the op obviously, so Miriam stayed with her. But the baby's beautiful, Mae. A lovely big boy, which was no doubt the cause of the problem as she's small like Miriam. Jonas is over the moon, of course. He adores Precious as she's his last child and only daughter, so this grandson is going to be very special and spoiled, I think."

"What time did you get back?" Aunt Mae would not be satisfied until she had a clear picture of the whole night's events.

"About four o'clock this morning," Paddy said, stifling a yawn and rubbing his tired eyes.

"Jonas was waiting for us at the gate," Beth said with a laugh. "We'd called him straight away when the baby was safely born to tell him the news, but he wanted to hear the details. He was so thrilled. He's going to take the next few days off so he can go see them and help Matthew get ready for when they come home."

"Who's Matthew?"

"Precious' husband," Beth said patiently.

Satisfied that at last she had all the details of the night's adventure, Mae turned her attention to her breakfast for a few quiet minutes.

"We're going to Becky's for lunch today," Lori said presently.

"Oh dear, I'd clean forgotten about that in all the excitement," Beth said, turning to Paddy. "You won't be able to have a rest this afternoon, darling, and you're *so* tired."

"Yes, I will, actually," Paddy said with an apologetic smile. "Sorry sweetheart, I forgot to tell you. Becky called just before breakfast when I was in the office. She asked if we can come tomorrow rather than today."

"Oh." Beth looked surprised and then frowned. "Is she alright? Did she say why?"

"Yes, she's fine. I said you'd probably phone her after breakfast. I think Joe's busy on the farm, that's all. We agreed Saturday would be a better day for all of us."

"I suppose so," Beth said slowly. "Not quite sure why we decided on Friday to begin with. Never mind. I'll give her a call just now."

"I'd like to go and visit Precious and the baby," Lori said, "but today's probably too soon. How long will she be in hospital?"

"Probably a few days, because of the caesarian," Beth said, "but not many. They don't like to keep the women in too long; no room. I'll check with Jonas and we can either go in on Monday or see her when she's back home. I'll have some time then to prepare some things for the baby. I've got some lovely gifts put away, clothes and blankets and things."

There was a lull in the conversation and the room was quiet again, other than the scraping of butter-knife on toast and soft sipping of hot drinks. Until Carla, still in her robe and with her hair pulled back in an untidy pony-tail and blue smudges under her eyes, walked in.

"Hello darling. What are you doing up?" Beth asked. "I thought you'd sleep away the morning."

"No, sadly. I woke up. Need coffee," Carla mumbled, still sounding half asleep as she headed for the drinks tray at the end of the table. She poured herself a large mug of coffee and plopped into an empty chair.

"Right," Lori said, folding her napkin and standing up. "I'm going to make a quiche to take to Becky's tomorrow. You should go and have a rest, Mum. You look exhausted." Collecting her own plates and mug, she carried them out to the kitchen.

"And there goes Sister dearest," Carla muttered sarcastically as she started to slice and dice a large mango. "I enter a room, and she leaves it."

Mae stared at her niece with surprise. She'd seen Carla do exactly the same thing herself, several times before. She wanted to say something but knew it wasn't her place. Not right then, anyway.

"You're both as bad as each other," Paddy said crossly as he pushed his chair back and reached for his hat. "I'm getting really tired of the silliness between you two and wish you'd sort it out." He slapped his hat on his head with uncharacteristic force and almost forgot to give Beth his customary kiss before exiting the room.

"Somebody's grouchy," Carla said as she continued to dissect the mango.

"He's just tired, dear," Beth said. "More coffee sweetheart?"

"Oh, for goodness' sake," Mae muttered under her breath and landed a well-aimed kick on Beth's ankle.

"Ow!" Beth said, frowning at Mae. "What did you do that for?"

Mae pursed her lips and jabbed her head in Carla's direction. Beth had just missed an ideal opportunity to share some hard truths with Carla who munched her fruit, seemingly oblivious to the interaction between her aunt and mother.

"Were you offering more coffee?" Carla asked without looking up. "Yes please Mum, I'd love another cup."

Mae sighed, shook her head in disappointment at her sister's aversion for confrontation, and began to stack her own used plates.

"I'll go see if Lori needs any help," she said with a pointed look at Beth and scraped her chair back clumsily just as Lori came back into the dining room.

"Should I use this butter for the pastry, Mum?" Lori asked, picking up the butter dish from the table.

Beth opened her mouth to answer but Carla spoke first.

"Lori," she said, her tone casual. "Where is Nana Lily's ring?"

"What?" Lori seemed completely taken aback by this direct and unexpected question and looked enquiringly at her mother. Beth shrugged but shot a panicked look at Mae.

"Nana . . . Lily's . . . ring," Carla repeated as if speaking to someone who was hard of hearing or understanding. "Dad gave it to you years ago before you left to go traipsing around the world. Where is it? You never wear it. Have you lost it?"

Lori found her tongue. "Of course I haven't lost it!" she snapped.

"So where is it? Why don't you ever wear it?" Carla asked, looking up at Lori.

"I don't have to explain anything to you," Lori said through her teeth and turned to leave the room. But Mae was by the door and gently caught her arm.

"What's this all about, girls? What's this ring?"

"Nana Lily's ring," Carla said. "The most beautiful ring you can imagine. Well, *I* think so. It should have been mine; Nana Lily promised, but Daddy—with his sense of tradition that can never be broken—gave it to Lori who never liked or appreciated it like I did."

Mae was intrigued. "Lori?"

"I do, I love it," Lori protested, looking distressed. "It's beautiful and precious because it belonged to Nana. But it doesn't fit me, Aunt Mae, and I don't want to have it altered. So, I . . . I keep it safe."

"I can't *believe* it! What a waste. I knew Daddy shouldn't have given it to you." Carla was close to tears.

"Be grateful I haven't cut it up and had it made into something else," Lori hissed, making Carla gasp at the awful thought.

"It really is the most beautiful ring, Mae," Beth said quickly, "and such a romantic story."

Mae knew her sister was trying to diffuse the situation, and was curious to hear the backstory to the ring. She remembered seeing Lily Maguire wearing it; one didn't forget a piece of jewelry like that. "Goody, another story," she said taking her seat. "Do tell, Beth."

"Well, Paddy's father, Patrick Senior, had it made for Lily when he was courting her. She was such a beautiful, refined young lady that he was sure she'd never exchange Ireland for a lonely corner of Africa. But his heart was set on her, so he went to great expense to have a special ring made for her in the shape of a lily."

Carla picked up the tale. "The centerpiece is a halo of diamond petals encircling the most *exquisite* diamond, Aunt Mae. And then there's a whole host of tiny diamonds set in rose gold that twist in a wreath with overlapping leaves on either side of the flower. It's stunning." Her eyes began to brim with tears. "She'd let me wear it sometimes, if I sat very close to her and was careful not to drop it. The best was at night-time, before bed. It looked especially beautiful in candlelight, so Nana would light one next to my bed and I'd lie there, turning it this way and that to see all the sparkling rainbow colors."

"Patrick's uncle was a jeweler," Beth said, "and apparently a renowned expert at cutting diamonds so all their facets would catch the light in the most wonderful way. It's a very valuable piece of jewelry and I think the only one Lily allowed herself to keep when she came out to Africa."

"She was such a *lovely* lady, wasn't she?" Mae said. "So elegant. I did like her enormously."

"Very gentle and caring as well, but with the most incredible strength," Beth said. "She didn't have an easy life, as you can imagine. Patrick Senior was a hard man and totally married to his work. But she never complained, and she adored her boys."

"Especially Daddy," Lori said.

"Yes, especially Paddy," Beth agreed. "He was the most like her."

"And Carla was her favorite grandchild," Lori said matter-of-factly.

"Yes," Beth said, "they really did share a special bond."

Mae knew the story but Beth told it anyway. Carla evidently looked very much like Lily's little sister who'd died of influenza at a young age. As soon as she'd seen baby Carla with her shock of dark red hair, smooth, pale skin and blue-green, slightly slanted eyes, she'd been captivated and quickly became utterly devoted to the child.

In the last years of her life, Lily had become a frequent guest at Kalulu Ranch, coming to stay at least several times a year for a few weeks and sometimes months at a time, especially after Paddy's father passed away. She and Carla would spend hours together, reading or walking around the garden as Lily taught Carla about all the different plants and insects they'd see on their explorations. Sometimes, they'd just sit together and chat or read, Carla on a little stool near Lily's feet, her arms on the grand old lady's knees, pointed chin resting in her hands as she gazed adoringly at her beautiful Nana.

As Beth talked on fondly about her mother-in-law, Mae watched her nieces. Carla fiddled with her napkin ring, the odd tear running unchecked down her cheeks as she listened to her mother. Lori sat very quiet and still, gazing at Carla with a look of deep sadness. Was it regret? Mae couldn't be sure.

Lori's eyes suddenly shifted and caught her aunt's stare, and whatever it was Mae thought she'd seen there vanished.

Chapter 9

As Lori joined her family for lunch in the coolness of the creeper-shaded verandah, she heard a diesel-engine vehicle crunch to a stop in the driveway, its door bang shut, and the sound of footsteps approaching the house. She wasn't surprised when she heard the deep voice calling out at the front door.

"Hello?"

"We're out here, Jake," she called.

"Come join us for lunch," Beth said.

"Don't mind if I do, if it's okay with you," Jake said with a broad grin as he appeared around the side of the house.

"You're always welcome, dear," Beth said as Lori went to fetch extra plates and cutlery.

"Thank you. I'll just wash up and be back in a second."

"Back from the *boma*?" Paddy asked a few minutes later while Jake, now seated next to Lori, cut himself a couple of thick slices of homemade bread.

"Yeah, had some things to do there this morning."

"Who did you see there this time?" Lori asked. A trip to the *boma* was always a good opportunity for farmers to see distant neighbors and have a few minutes' conversation before continuing with their business.

"Funny you should ask," he said. "I saw Hugh and Rose in the bank. D'you know them? Apparently, they heard you're out for a bit and asked me to send you their special greetings. Say they can't wait to meet you."

Lori's brow crinkled in thought as she sipped her lemonade. "Is that the couple from Zimbabwe? They moved here since I was last out, didn't they? So, no, I've never met them."

"That's them," Paddy said. "Lost their farm in Zimbabwe so moved up and took over the Carters' farm on the far side."

"Lovely couple," Beth said, passing the potato salad to Mae. "She's actually from South Africa and an absolute sweetie. Ever since they heard you live in Israel, they always ask us about you, every time we see them."

"Now you mention it," Paddy said, "Robert was also interested to hear that you were coming out, Lori. I told him you'd probably see him at the church picnic next week."

"Robert? Do I know him?"

"Probably not. He's only been here about a year or so. Manages for Jack and Carol Tanner. Came out pretty green from England so I didn't think he'd hang around very long, but he's doing well."

Lori smiled. She was always pleased to meet new people and share her point of view about the country where she lived. Especially those who had a heart for Israel or at least were prepared to talk and listen without bias, which was sadly not always the case.

"I actually saw the Tanners this morning," Jake said, "Carol told me you had an adventurous night." He grinned across the table at Carla.

"You're kidding," Carla said. "Wow, talk about wildfire."

"I hear you put your nursing skills to good use."

"Not really. Poor Precious had to have a C-section in the end, so I wasn't able to help much."

Lori looked hard at Carla. Was she being coy or genuinely playing down her part in the previous night's drama?

"Remember I told you last time you were here that I'm building a clinic with my neighbors?" Jake asked Carla. "It's on my farm but it'll be for all our workers and their families, and anyone else in the area for that matter."

"Ja, I remember." Carla nodded. "You showed me the plans on my last visit."

"Well, it took a while but we finished it last week. All the equipment's in and everything." He paused and laying down his knife and fork, looked directly at Carla. "I wondered if you'd like to come over and see it."

Lori froze, only her gaze darting between Jake and Carla. His invitation was directed at Carla, to the exclusion of everyone else at the table; that was obvious. She was even more horrified to see Carla's cheeks flush a little as she smiled directly back at Jake.

"I'd love to see it," she said. "We can go straight after lunch, if you want."

Jake beamed. "Sounds good."

"I'd like to come too!" Lori's outburst sounded a little shrill, even to herself, and was followed by an awkward silence.

Carla glared at Lori. "You go then." Her tone was icy. "I'll go another time. I'm tired anyway."

"But I need your nurse's opinion, Carla," Jake said, "and I want to show you the maternity suite. It's pretty impressive. Please come."

He is pleading with her, Lori thought with a twinge of disgust.

"Go on, Carla," Beth said. "Jake's been dying to show it off to you ever since the last brick was laid. You can have an early night instead."

Carla looked at Jake for a long moment. "Alright," she sighed.

"Good," Jake said, beaming. "You won't be disappointed, I promise."

Lori knew that she should tactfully back down; that would be the adult thing to do. But somehow, she just couldn't. And besides, she felt she had every right to go. She was proud of Jake for making this substantial investment that would benefit so many people in the area, most of whom didn't have easy access, physical or financial, to such a facility. She wanted to see it for herself and give him the confirmation he deserved. The fact that in tagging along she'd be irritating Carla was just an added bonus.

"I'll get some cool drinks," Jake said over his shoulder as he made his way toward the kitchen, tossing his hat onto one of the lounge chairs as he passed. "What would you like?" he called. "Water? Juice? Beer?"

"Juice, please," Lori said. "Your water still tastes weird to me."

"Juice is fine for me, too," Carla said.

He was pleased. The tour of the clinic had been a success, not least because Lori and Carla were vaguely civil to each other. They'd both seemed suitably impressed, and Carla had given a lot of practical advice as well as glowing praise. He'd then proudly driven them around his well-organized and tidy farm until they'd ended up at his house for a drink before he took them back home.

"This was the manager's house, wasn't it, Jake?" Lori asked from the lounge. "What was his name again?"

"Barclay," Jake answered as he peered into the fridge. "John Barclay. He married and bought his own farm a couple of hours north of here. Left about ten years ago when I came back from the States, so I moved in here." He carried the tray of three glasses filled with ice and a jug full of lemon juice into the lounge. "I've always liked this corner of the farm. It's close to the river and the folks' house still feels too big for me right now. But you've been here before."

"Yeah, I have. Brought the kids for a braai a couple of times on previous visits. Just couldn't remember the name of the guy who used to live here before." Lori walked over to the mantelpiece above the fireplace.

"Lori, come; let's sit outside on the verandah," Jake said in an effort to steer her attention away from what he knew could completely change the positive tone of the visit they'd enjoyed up until that moment.

But he was too late. She'd already picked up the framed photograph and was staring down at it, running her finger across the three innocent young faces that grinned up at her from behind the glass. He knew she was familiar with the picture and had at least one copy of her own.

She clasped it to her chest and followed him out to the verandah. Dropping onto the scruffy wicker couch next to Jake, Lori stood the photograph on the coffee table opposite them and took the glass he held out to her.

"Thanks," she said. "Yum. This brings back memories."

"Mom's recipe of home-made juice from the same, faithful old trees."

"*L'haim*, to life." Lori smiled as she clinked her glass against Jake's. "How are they, Sadie and Terry?"

"Pretty good, actually. You know Mom turned my grandfather's stud farm into a riding school for people with special needs."

"Yes, Mum told me. Suits her down to the ground. What an amazing lady."

"Well, she's loving that, and Dad potters around. He has to take it slowly now he has a heart condition. But he's okay. I speak to them pretty often. Dad still demands frequent reports about what's going on here."

"Give them my love please."

"Will do." Jake knew that Lori was very fond of his parents. "They'd loved to have been here for your Mom's party. They still miss Africa and all their friends like crazy, especially your folks. But the doctor wouldn't give Dad the green light, and Mom didn't want to leave him on his own."

"That's a shame," Lori said.

They sat in silence for a while, their eyes inevitably drawn back to the photograph on the table in front of them.

"There isn't a day that goes by I don't miss him," Jake said at last. "Sometimes, I even catch myself talking to him. And then I think I must be going nuts." There was no need to mention his name; Lori would know he was talking about Tom.

"No, no, you're not," she said. "I do that too."

"The best is when I dream about him. That's great, like old times. But it doesn't happen so often anymore, which scares me. Like I'm forgetting him." He paused. "How can that be, Lor?"

She took his hand and squeezed it. "You're not forgetting him, Jake."

He looked out to the garden beyond the verandah. He'd purposefully kept it very simple, the kikuyu grass lawn stretching down to an expanse of beautiful Zambian bush trees under which snaked a sandy path down to the small river. As they sat quietly for a few moments, they could hear its burbling flow.

"I have a recurring dream. In fact, I had it just a couple of weeks ago. We were playing pooh-sticks on the bridge," she said, smiling up at Jake. "D'you remember how we used to play that?"

"Sure do."

"In my dream, you broke his stick by throwing a stone into the water."

"He'd probably broken mine the round before." Jake chuckled.

"Yes, probably." Lori fell silent again for a few moments.

"Tell me more."

"It was so strange," she said in little more than a whisper. "He spoke to me, in the dream, you know . . . and it was so real."

She looked up at Jake and he saw for the millionth time, with a raw ache, how like his friend—the only 'brother' he'd ever had—she was, except for the sadness crouching like a shadow in her eyes. Tom's eyes had never had that shadow; he'd never known the grief his twin sister carried since that fateful day.

Lori opened her mouth but whatever she was going to say remained unsaid.

"I dream of Tom."

Lori spun around. "How could you possibly? You were only a baby when he died."

Jake was shocked at the vehemence of Lori's tone and stare with which she'd fixed her sister, and at the same time full of admiration for Carla who stood her ground.

"I was five, and I do," Carla said.

Moving away from the doorway behind them where she'd been standing, she sat on the low verandah wall, facing Jake and Lori. She pulled her hair over one shoulder and twisted it as she spoke. "Strange, but it's also a recurring dream. I've figured out I have it when I'm a bit stressed," she said, looking at Jake.

"What is it?" Jake felt bad that he and Lori had slipped off into their 'Tom-space' as they called it, to the exclusion of his second, very important guest. Although he was acutely aware of the explosive atmosphere, he still wanted to encourage Carla.

Carla stared at a trail of tiny ants making their way, single-file, over the rough cement floor of the verandah. She looked a bit pale, Jake thought. Perhaps she won't tell her story after all; that would be best. But instead she took a deep breath, raised her chin and persevered despite her apparent misgivings.

"It's like I'm very small and helpless, at least I feel helpless," she said. "I'm in water; it's deep and dark where I am but I look up and see light way above me. I'm afraid, but just as I'm floating deeper into the nothingness below, Tom appears in front of me. He reaches out, grabs hold of me and pulls me up toward the light. His face is close to mine. He smiles his beautiful smile and I'm not afraid anymore. He says something, but I can't understand his words; I'm just fascinated by the bubbles floating out of his mouth and I follow them up to the light."

Carla looked up at the verandah ceiling of cane-reed mats, as if she saw the bubbles floating there, and then over her shoulder to the garden behind. Jake stared at her in astonishment. He felt rather like a mesmerized rabbit, aware of impending disaster but paralyzed and so helpless to avert it. He was aware of Lori's labored breathing beside him and willed Carla to stop, but she didn't.

"I've talked about it with my boss, Max," she continued, "as I wanted to hear what he thought about it. It's not difficult to understand, really. Whenever I reach a dark and unhappy or lonely place, my big brother's there to pull me out of it, just as he would if he were still alive." She paused, her gaze on the ants at her feet again. "Things always seem to work out okay after I've had the dream. It's uncanny," she finished with a smile, finally looking up to face Jake and Lori.

Jake, stunned by what he'd heard, saw Carla's smile freeze and the blood drain from her face. Following her gaze, he looked at Lori beside him. She sat rigid and ashen as if she'd seen a ghost, her eyes huge under raised brows, her mouth open in disbelief. No-one said anything for a long and awful moment.

Gradually, Lori's face darkened into an ominous scowl. She stood up and walked behind the couch. Carla winced, almost cowering, as if afraid that Lori would strike her, but Lori walked straight past her and started down the steps. Half way down, she turned around and glowered at Jake.

"Don't you tell her, Jake Hamilton," she growled. "Don't you *dare* tell her."

Before Jake had time to react or stop her, she'd run down the remaining steps, across the lawn and out the gate.

"Lori!" Jake jumped down the steps and started across the lawn after her. "Lor, come on, come back." But she was already a hundred meters along the dirt farm road leading away from his house. She was fit and had always been the better runner; there was no point in even trying to catch her on foot. Besides, it was probably better to leave her alone. She'd run home and hopefully be calmer by the time she got there. He'd give her the space she needed, he decided, turning back to the house with a deep sigh.

"Jake?" Carla, visibly shaken, was standing on the top step, looking down at him. "What just happened? What can't you tell me?"

Jake stopped at the foot of the steps. He shook his head and then took a deep breath and looked up at Carla, the beautiful young woman whom he knew with a deep certainty was the love of his life. He shook his head again.

"I'm sorry, Carla," he said, walking slowly up the steps as if carrying a huge weight. "You're going to have to talk to Lori about it."

"It's bad, it's something bad," Carla said, her eyes beginning to fill with tears.

Jake put his arms around her and held her close, mindful of her head on his shoulder and her tears dampening his shirt. He couldn't think of anything comforting to say, so he said nothing at all.

Lori ran as if her life depended on it. The adjacent Hamilton and Maguire farms had been her childhood playground so she was easily able to navigate her way back home, hardly conscious of the paths she was taking. She was aware only of the need to keep putting one leg in front of the other, the puffs of sand kicked up by her sneakers, the sound of her rhythmic breathing, the trickle of sweat down the side of her face, and the necessity to put as much distance as possible between herself, her sister, and what had just taken place at Jake's house.

As she neared home, she knew she couldn't face her parents. Veering off the path, she ran towards the only place she could bear to be. She pushed through the gate of the hedged garden and collapsed on the grassy slope beside Tom's grave. She lay where she fell, her unseeing eyes skyward, her chest heaving with the exertion of the run and the huge sobs fighting their way up from deep inside her.

One chink in the emotional dam wall she'd unwittingly built over the years, and it had all come crashing down. This time—perhaps for the first time—she didn't try to stop the flood, but instead let the pain of it fill her body until every nerve ending seemed to be on fire. She turned her face to the grass and pummeled it with her fist.

"*Why God, why?*" she cried over and over again.

She heard Aunt Mae calling her name, the clang of the gate, and then felt her there, close beside her, stroking her hair. Slowly, the physical pain began to subside, her sobs reduced to occasional shuddering sighs, and Lori raised herself enough to crawl into Aunt Mae's arms and lay motionless against her. She didn't feel the need to explain herself and her aunt asked no questions.

They sat together in silence until the grass grew damp and the sky was sponged with sunset colors. Lori sat up and wiped the last of the wet off her face with her hands.

"Oh, my darling," Mae said tenderly. "My heart breaks for you."

"Thank you, Aunt Mae," Lori said as she stood up slowly. She felt stiff all over and her legs were wobbly.

"Well, sweetheart, I don't quite know how I made it down onto the ground, but you're going to have to get me up again."

Mae was not only older but substantially heavier than her sister Beth. She started to giggle as she rolled onto her knees, her bottom pointed skywards.

"Don't laugh, Auntie. You'll go weak and then we won't be able to get you back on your feet at all." This situation would normally have had Lori in stitches of laughter but now she could hardly muster a smile. She took hold of a chubby arm and braced herself. "There you go," she grunted, heaving her aunt to her feet.

"Thank you darling, very kind of you," Aunt Mae said and made her way over to the bench on the far side of the grave. "How beautiful it always is in here, and peaceful. I haven't been in here yet this visit. Have you?"

Lori nodded. "Every day."

Mae patted the empty space on the bench beside her. "Come sit with me a bit."

Obediently Lori sat beside her. "How did you know I was here?" she asked eventually, her tone flat.

"Jake called, and when you didn't come to the house Beth thought you might be here."

Lori nodded slowly. "And yet *you* came to find me . . ."

"Oh, that was my idea, dear. Don't be upset with your Mum."

Lori shook her head. She wasn't upset; she understood.

They sat in silence, each lost in her own thoughts in the evening tranquility of the enclosed garden. Lori watched a tiny bird hovering over the flowers on either side of the gravestone until it flew over the tall hedge and disappeared into the gathering darkness.

"How do you do it, you and Mum?" Lori said suddenly.

"Do what, dear?"

"Be best friends and companions, and love each other like you do, even though you live so far apart from each other."

"Oh," Aunt Mae said, "well, we weren't always like that."

Lori turned to fix her with a surprised stare. "Really?"

Aunt Mae chuckled. "We used to fight like a couple of cats sometimes," she said. "But as children, we usually managed to keep our mother's rule of never going to bed angry. We'd always hug and say sorry before the day was done, even if we didn't particularly feel like it."

"Usually?"

"I can only remember one time that we didn't talk for a few days. Oh, my goodness, that was awful. We were both devastated but as stubborn as old mules."

"What happened?"

"It was about Beth following your dad out here to Africa. I was terrified for her and didn't want her to go, but she'd made up her mind and refused to hear anything negative about it. I understood later that she was just as frightened, if not more so, but we were both so proud."

"How did you fix it?"

"Oh, it didn't take long. After two or three days, we couldn't stand it anymore. We tried to put ourselves in each other's shoes—another of our darling mother's wise methods—so we understood where we were both coming from. I was just being selfish. She didn't want to leave me either, but if she hadn't come out after Paddy, she would have missed out on her love story. I had to let her go."

"So, you made peace."

"Yes, of course we did," Aunt Mae said. "The thing to realize, dear, is that family have fights all the time." She paused for a few seconds and looked closely at her niece. "But we still need each other," she added gently.

Lori was silent for a long time.

"Let's go inside and I'll make you a nice cup of tea," Aunt Mae suggested eventually, tea being her remedy for all ills.

Lori stood. "No, thanks. I think I'd rather be alone this evening, so I'll shower and go to bed."

She picked up a little stone and added it to the little pile already resting on her brother's grave, then turned to look directly at Aunt Mae. "Thanks for not asking."

Aunt Mae nodded and took Lori's hand as they left the garden, the gate clanging shut behind them. "That's alright sweetheart. But I'm here for you, whenever you do feel the need to talk."

Lori nodded, but no longer had the energy or desire to reply. It was almost completely dark and all she wanted to do was sleep, so that she could forget about the whole awful day.

Chapter 10

"The weather's been strange lately," Lori said. "Grey and cloudy early this morning and now it's turned into the most gorgeous day."

"Yes, it's lovely, isn't it?" Beth looked out the car window at a deep blue sky dotted with white puffballs of cloud.

"A few days ago, it was the complete opposite," Lori said. "Beautiful morning and spitting rain in the afternoon. I don't remember April being like this. Thought the rainy season was over."

"It is," Paddy said, slowing down to navigate a deep dip in the dirt road leading to Joe and Becky's farm. "But April's been like this for the last two or three years. In fact, last year we had a huge electric storm in the middle of the month. Remember that, Beth? Blew out our telly and my computer. Worse still, the crops shouldn't be getting a wetting at this stage."

"Oh, my goodness, yes. That was a bad one. You should have seen the lightning," Beth said, glancing over her shoulder to the three back-seat passengers. Lori sat behind Paddy, the quiche in its covered pie-dish balanced on her knees; Aunt Mae was wedged in between her and Carla, who hadn't said a word the whole trip.

Beth gazed out at the roadside with their pretty masses of tall, wild, yellow daisies and lilac foxgloves amid swaying, fuzzy, pink-topped molasses grass. Her hands rested on the tin containing the large chocolate cake she'd made that morning even though Becky had told her not to bother. Lunch out was always a treat for her, but today she was particularly looking forward to what she wished would be at least a diversion and hopefully a dilution of the increasing tension between Lori and Carla.

She thought back to the previous afternoon. She and Mae had been having tea in the *lapa* when Jake called, so they were on the lookout for Lori. She didn't come back to the house but Beth had thought she'd heard the noise of the gate to Tom's garden. It was good that Mae had gone to speak to Lori; she was so much better at those things. She had wanted to go herself, but somehow, she couldn't. Why not? That question had robbed her of sleep for most of the night. She suddenly felt very tired.

"That magnificent old tree is still standing," Lori said as they neared the river.

On the right-hand side of the road, just before the bridge, an enormous tree gripped the riverbank at a precarious angle, its large roots reaching for the water.

Its thick trunk was gnarled and twisted and its heavy, long branches spread out in all directions, some hung with untidy nests.

"I don't like the look of it at all," Paddy said, slowing down as he drove past it so as to have a closer look. "I've told Joe if it gets knocked over in a storm, it'll fall right onto the bridge. But Becky won't hear of it being cut down."

"Just like she won't hear about having a concrete bridge built instead of this rickety old thing," Beth said, raising her voice to be heard over the clacking racket of the car's wheels on wooden planks as they crossed the bridge. Nervously, she peered over the edge to the dark-green waters of the river flowing beneath it.

"Why ever not?" Aunt Mae asked as the vehicle bumped over the end of the bridge and surged up the rise toward Becky and Joe's home.

"The sound of the wooden planks reminds Becky of those old bridges up where Nana and Granda Maguire used to live," Lori said with a smile. "Brings back childhood memories, she says."

"That's our Becky," Paddy said as he drew up by the side of the house. Three large dogs rushed out to greet them followed by Joe, Ben, and Riley.

"Hi, welcome," Joe said over the din. "Down, Caesar, down!" He grabbed the largest dog by its collar and opened the car door for Lori. "Don't mind them," he said. "They look ferocious but you know they're quite useless, really."

"I don't mind a bit," Lori said, patting the massive head of one of the Rottweilers while holding the quiche aloft. "You're really a big softy, aren't you?" she cooed at the dog, which was now wagging his tail madly and drooling all over her shoes. "That's one of Rex's daughters, isn't it?" she asked, pointing at a beautiful female German shepherd.

"Ja, that's Zena, Becky's adoring shadow," Joe said. "She's a lovely dog."

"Hello my gorgeous boys. Come give your Gran a kiss," Beth said. "Why don't you take the cake for me, Ben? That's very kind."

They all followed Joe through a rose-twisted arch set in a thick hedge that gave the house privacy and protection from the dust of arriving vehicles, and up stone steps onto a wide verandah.

The house itself was a long, low bungalow, its raw brick walls almost completely invisible beneath a scented floral creeper. The windows along the front of the house were huge, giving the full benefit of the view over the flower-filled garden and beyond to the field that sloped down to the river's edge.

As they entered the lounge through sliding doors, Becky appeared at the far end of the large room.

"Hi everybody, welcome," she said, wiping her hands on the apron tied above her bump. "Oh, Mum, I told you not to bother making a cake," she said, taking the tin from Ben and peeking inside. "But I'm glad you did as it looks amazing. We'll keep it for tea. Joe, sweetheart, will you do the drinks?"

Beth and Lori followed Becky into the kitchen.

"I made the quiche, as promised," Lori said, putting it down on the wooden table amongst the other bowls and serving dishes.

"Ah, thanks, Lor. Looks delicious. I decided to do a cold lunch of cut meats and salads with your quiche, and then a few yummy puddings."

"Sounds good, and it all looks great. Hello Flora, how are you?" Lori greeted Becky's housekeeper who turned from the stove to greet them as she spooned baked potatoes from sizzling baking pan to serving dish.

"Let's just carry all this into the dining room," Becky said, picking up a glass salad bowl. "And then Flora, you must go home. I have plenty of help now."

With the additional help, the buffet lunch was soon laid out on the sideboard in the dining room.

"What a wonderful room this is," Mae said, taking her place at the table. "I love the ethnic theme. I think I tell you this every time I come here but you really do have a lovely home, Becky."

"Thank you, Aunt Mae." Becky beamed.

"You do, Mae," Beth said with a wry smile. "But Becky never gets tired of hearing it." She knew that Becky was very house-proud and had worked hard on every room of her home over the years until she'd achieved the specific look and effect she'd envisioned. She deserved the praise.

Beth noticed an extra place set at the table. "Expecting someone else?" she asked.

"Yes," Joe answered. "We invited Jake to join us. Baked potato, Dad?"

Right on cue, the sound of a jeep and the dogs' raucous barking signaled his arrival.

"Hello?" called Jake from the lounge.

"In here, Jake."

"Hi all. Sorry I'm late." Jake appeared at the door looking very handsome in clean blue jeans and T-shirt rather than his usual farm work clothes. "Had a busy, grubby morning, so I preferred to clean up before coming over." He held out a bottle of wine. "Where should I put this?"

"Not a problem," Joe said taking the wine and handing him a plate. "Thanks for that. Help yourself to some grub and grab a seat."

"This all looks amazing, Becks. Far cry from my usual Saturday slim pickings." Jake set a heaping plate down at the empty place next to Carla, sat down, and grinned across the table at Lori. "Hello Titch."

"Didn't know we'd have the pleasure of *your* company," Lori said, slicing one of Becky's savory muffins in half.

"Wouldn't miss it for the world," Jake said, glancing at Carla.

"So, what did you decide to do with that far field, Joe?" Paddy asked, piling grated cheese onto a steaming baked potato.

"No farm talk at the table, Daddy. That's my rule," Becky said firmly. "Aunt Mae," she continued, ignoring her father's look of protest, "surely you have some funny stories about Dad in England that we haven't all heard yet."

"Indeed, I do," Mae said with a mischievous grin.

"Just remember, Mae," Paddy said waving his fork at her, "for every story you can tell about me, I have at least two or three worse ones about you."

Beth's prayers were answered and the luncheon was a relaxed and festive affair, largely thanks to Paddy and Mae's hilarious and richly embellished stories of times past.

"Let's take our coffee out onto the verandah," Becky said after they'd finished their desserts.

"Not sure if I can move after all that food," Paddy said.

"What about the dishes, Becks? I can go do those now."

"No, thanks Mum. We can stack them in the kitchen, and Joe and I can do them later. I just want to put my feet up for a while. Can't deal with them right now."

The party moved outdoors into the warm mid-afternoon sunshine, the adults plumping down into the verandah chairs, the boys begging to be allowed to swim.

"Absolutely not," Becky said. "It's too soon after lunch. You'll get cramps and your toes will curl."

Lori laughed. "That's what always used to happen to you."

"Who's for a walk?" Joe asked. "Or we can take a drive to our dam. I saw a pair of fish eagles out there yesterday."

"I'll take a rain check on that, son." Paddy settled back into a chair with a satisfied sigh. "I think I'm going to stay put. Might even have a bit of a snooze."

"Aunt Mae?"

"If you don't mind, I think I'll stay here too, dear. I'll come over another time to see your dam. I've heard it's gorgeous out there. Why don't the rest of you go and leave us oldies here? We'll have tea ready by the time you come back," she said.

"Oldies and fat pregnant ladies," Becky said.

"Aunt Lori, please come," Riley said, tugging on her arm. "You promised you'd come see the bike track we made. Dad, Dad, please can we go show them the bike track?"

"Sure, we'll go see the track and then onto the dam."

Joe led the way to his open-back truck, boys and dogs hot on his heels, Carla and Jake deep in discussion behind them. They had hardly stopped chatting together since Jake had arrived, Lori thought, as she walked behind them. Suddenly Carla tripped on the uneven ground of the dirt parking space but Jake caught her, preventing her from falling. Lori couldn't help but notice that he held her a few seconds longer than he needed to. They seemed frozen in time, gazing at each other until Carla flushed, ducking her head and turning toward the car. He didn't let go of her hand.

"Aunt Lori, please come in the back with us."

Lori shook her head, trying to dislodge the unsettling scenes from her thoughts. "Sure, Riley," she said, trying to muster a smile for her nephew. "Doesn't look like there'll be room for me in the front anyway," she muttered to herself as she climbed in and sat with her back against the hard metal siding.

"Are you okay there, Lor?" Jake asked, holding the door of the single cab open while Carla climbed in and slid across to the middle. "I can sit there in back, and you come into the cab."

"No, I'm fine, thanks," Lori snapped. Irritated with herself for her tell-tale tone, she turned her attention to the boys. "Now, tell me all about your bike track."

Jake climbed in next to Carla and Joe drove up the road away from the house and river. They passed a long, narrow field of closely cropped grass with a windowless single-story building at its far end. A billowing wind sock marked the field as Joe's runway; his six-seater plane safely housed in the hangar at its end. A pilot's license and small aircraft were very useful things for a farmer in these parts, and Lori knew Joe had been diligent about obtaining both as soon as the couple could afford it.

In the bumpy back of the truck, Ben and Riley chatted to Lori about how they'd built the bike track in a patch of bush beyond the airfield and their plans for holding a race day there, perhaps even sometime during these holidays. Lori tried to listen but her eyes were drawn again and again to the sight through the cabin's back window of Jake's arm around Carla's shoulder. At one point, Carla had laid her head against his shoulder and the expression on Jake's face as he had looked down at her made Lori turn away quickly. She'd never seen him looking at anyone like that before. But then again, she wasn't here very often to see.

"There it is, Aunt Lori. There's the track."

Joe slowed to a stop and they all piled out to inspect and admire the results of the boys' hard work: the ramps, hairpin bends and obstacles.

"Did you guys build all this yourselves?" Carla asked. "It's really impressive."

"Well," Riley said, "Dad did help us quite a bit."

Joe ruffled his son's hair. "But it was all your design. I just did what I was told."

"I'd like to have a bash at this on a motorbike," Jake said.

Joe grinned. "You're on. We'll have a couple of practice runs and if it rides well, we'll turn it into a competition."

"Ah, cool! Really, Dad? Can we try too?" Ben's eyes shone with excitement.

"I don't think your mother would be too happy with me if I said yes, so that's going to have to be a no, son. At least until Jake and I have checked how it rides."

"I reckon it'll be much more fun to race your bicycles around," Lori said, seeing the disappointment in her nephews' fallen faces. "I'd love to do that with you, if you have a bike my size."

"Brilliant idea," Jake said. "We'll make a day of it. I have to be here to see you boys beat your aunt hollow. Carla, how are your bike riding skills?"

"Oh, wouldn't you just love to see me measure my length on one of these crazy bends," she said and laughed.

Lori walked around the track with the boys for a bit and made all the right noises but remained uneasy and distracted, so when it came time to drive on to the dam, she made her excuses.

"Joe, I'm going to walk back to the house, if you don't mind. Sorry, but I'm not feeling so good."

"Are you alright?" Joe asked. "I'll drive you back. These guys can start walking to the dam."

"No, no, I'm fine. Don't spoil your afternoon. I've just got a bit of a headache, that's all. Sorry boys," she added to her nephews. "Have fun and I'll see you back at home."

"Lor, wait. I'll walk you back," Jake called after her.

Lori was already several paces down the dirt road in the direction from where they'd come. "Wouldn't hear of it," she called and waved in response to Jake's offer but didn't turn around. She was relieved when she heard the sound of the vehicle retreating.

And then it hit her, for the second time in two days: a massive wave of anger twisting her stomach into painful knots. She felt as though she could hardly breathe and most annoyingly, tears stung her eyes. *Why? Why?* She screamed inside her head.

Yesterday, her outburst that had shocked her to the core had been because of Carla. Today, she was furious with Jake. She realized she was angrier with him than she'd ever been in all the years of their friendship. And disappointed. Yes, deeply disappointed. That was it.

What is *wrong* with me? She gripped the sides of her head with her finger-tips. Do I have any right to be angry? She shook her head vehemently as if to dislodge the tiny voice of self-doubt presumptuously echoing inside her. I do, of course I do. Why would he choose Carla, of all people?

She gradually calmed down as she walked, and started noticing the sights and sounds and smells around her as she kept a brisk pace down the bush road. Although they didn't delight her as they normally would, her anger began to fade. In its place, the tiny voice deep within her began to grow into a full-blown sense of guilty confusion.

Why was she feeling like this? Why did the thought of Jake and Carla upset her so? It wasn't jealousy, she was sure about that. She was a happily married wife and mother, and she'd long wanted Jake to have a wife and family of his own. She was being ridiculous and would have to pull herself together. It would be easier, though, if she could figure out *why* she was so terribly averse to the budding romance between her youngest sister and best friend.

Back at the house, she let herself in through the kitchen door, making sure it didn't bang shut in case anyone was having a snooze. She considered doing the dishes for Becky, but hearing voices from the direction of the verandah, thought better of it. Feeling hot and sticky after her fast-paced walk, she washed her hands at the sink, drank a glass of cold water from the fridge and then went through the lounge to join the rest of the party. But as she neared the open sliding doors, the words she overheard stopped her in her tracks.

"Lori had her life blown to pieces when Tom died." A soft breeze carried her father's deep voice into the lounge.

Lori instinctively pulled back into the corner beside the open doors and froze. Her back against the cold wall, she listened to the voices. Her instincts told her she shouldn't, but she couldn't help herself.

"We all did, Dad," Becky said quietly.

"No, no, not like that," Paddy said. "He was her twin," he added after a moment of silence. "They had always been inseparable. As toddlers, they had their own language. Remember that Beth? We were told it's not unusual for twins. It was fascinating to watch, their almost telepathic communication. They were kindred spirits. He was her world. And then he disappeared from her life and she was devastated. It changed her. She was just fifteen, a difficult age for any child. A teenager. She's never been the same since."

Paddy spoke haltingly, as if struggling with the memory of it all, and Lori was crushed. He'd lost his only son, but now he spoke as if he'd lost both his eldest children in one cruel blow.

"Carla was just a tiny girl, a precious, laughing little five-year-old," Beth said. "She knew something was wrong. She used to ask for Tom sometimes which was just heartbreaking. She didn't understand why he'd gone to heaven, why he didn't come and play with her anymore." Beth's voice caught in her throat and she was quiet for a little while. Lori knew she was trying to compose herself before she spoke again. "They both loved to play with her, Tom and Lori, from when she was a small baby. They'd make noises and funny faces just to make her laugh. She had the most infectious gurgling chuckle, like every baby I suppose."

"Lori never played with Carla again, after the accident," Paddy said. "She resisted every attempt we made to help rebuild their relationship over the years. At first it made me angry. I couldn't understand. It was so cruel. But then I eventually realized it was just too painful for Lori. There's only so much a person can bear."

"But Carla didn't understand why Lori didn't want anything to do with her anymore," Beth went on. "The poor little thing tried and tried to connect with her for a while and would be so upset when Lori pushed her away or ignored her. It was very distressing to watch. We didn't know what to do. Nothing we said could persuade Lori to behave any differently. She totally retreated into herself. Now I can see she should have gone into therapy or something, not that we had anybody around these parts then who could have helped her. The headmistress at her school knew what had happened, but we didn't speak to her about what was going on at home." Beth gave a deep, trembling sigh. "We were all grieving so terribly. It was such an *awful* time."

They were all silent for a few minutes. Someone sniffed and then blew their nose and Paddy cleared his throat gruffly.

Lori heard it all. She leant against the inner wall as they spoke, her eyes closed, her cheeks now wet. In their silence she opened her eyes and swiped at the tears with her hands in an attempt to get a grip on herself. She was about to tiptoe back in the direction of the kitchen when Beth spoke again.

"Eventually, Carla stopped trying," she said. "She started to totally ignore Lori, as if she'd consciously cut her out of her little life, in self-defense I suppose, poor darling. Remarkable, really. You never stopped trying to fix things, Becky; you found it very upsetting and always tried to keep the peace. But after a while, your father and I decided to just pray and let them be. We were convinced things would right themselves after a while. But they never did."

"We failed them." Paddy's voice was low and full of grief. "We failed you all. But we were grieving too. We were broken, your Mum and I. We'd lost our only son. With hindsight it's easy to see that we didn't handle the situation with you girls very well at all."

"Paddy," Beth said softly, "We did the best we could at the time, love. These memories are so horrendously painful that even though they are always there, somewhere close to the surface, we've tried not to dwell on them. But Becky asked, and she has a right to know."

"Don't beat yourself up about it, Dad," Becky said. Lori could tell from her voice that she was also crying. "It's not your or Mum's fault."

Everyone was quiet again.

"I'm sure Carla doesn't even remember why she pulled away from Lori," Becky said at last in a more composed tone. "She probably doesn't have any conscious recollection of all this, and yet she continues to behave almost as though Lori doesn't exist. At the same time, I don't think Lori remembers what caused the rift between them. She thinks it's Carla's fault while really, it's hers."

Lori felt as though she had been punched in the stomach. She wanted to run away, far away, but she felt glued to the spot.

"You can't blame them, Becky," Beth said. She sounded reproving.

"No, Mum, I'm not blaming either of them for what they did as heart-broken and confused children," Becky said. "But it's ridiculous that it's been allowed to go on for so long. They should both be made to understand what happened between them. They should know the root cause of their hatred or dislike or whatever it is they have for each other so that they can put it all behind them and move on. I want to go back to being a happy family again, like we used to be. Maybe it's a childish dream but I think we should at least try."

"It's not so easy, Becks," Paddy said. "We've tried talking to each of them on their previous visits here. But neither of them is even remotely interested in listening to what we have to say. They're both so *stubborn*." He chuckled. "No guesses as to where they got that from. But who knows? Maybe this time, it'll be different now they're here at home, together. It's been a long time since it all happened. With a lot of prayer and the magic of the old place, I believe things will come right between them."

"I agree," Beth said. "They'll not only make peace but be the best of friends, Becky, you'll see."

Becky laughed. "Oh, my goodness," she said. "I do love you two and your eternal optimism. But in fact, that's what I told Lori the other day, but I'm beginning to lose hope."

Aunt Mae spoke for the first time. "I'm inclined to agree with Becky although I don't think it's quite so funny. Perhaps you're being a little too optimistic, Bethy? You thought things would come right if they were left to their own devices in the past, but that didn't work, did it? Maybe having them under the same roof isn't enough."

"What are you saying, Mae? That we should just give up on them?"

"No, no, of course not, Beth. I think we should stage a kind of an *intervention*—force them into dealing with each other and solving their issues."

Lori frowned. Intervention?

"What do you think would make them do that, Mae?" Beth sounded surprised.

"I don't know but it's worth a try," Mae said. "They're not going to decide on their own to make peace and love each other again, and you really don't have any time to lose. Especially with the complication of Jake and Carla being romantically involved."

"What?" Beth said again. "No, no, silly; they're just good friends."

"Oh, my darling sister," Mae said. "Where have you *been*? They can't take their eyes off each other. I thought you knew by now."

"They've always just been the best of pals," Paddy said. "And besides, Carla's so much younger than him . . ." His voice trailed off. "Oh, good grief," he said after a small pause. "How on earth could we have been so obtuse?"

"You two must be the only ones around who haven't noticed," Mae said.

"Becky? Is this . . ."

"Yes Mum, it's true."

"Well I never," Beth said slowly. "I can't say I disapprove. Jake is already one of the family, and I always said he'd make someone the most wonderful husband one day. I just never thought it'd be our Carla. She's so settled in her life in Cape Town. I never *dreamed* she'd be willing to give all that up. Are you *sure*?"

"Yes, Mum, absolutely."

"Have you spoken to her about it?"

"No, not yet. Haven't had a chance," Becky said.

"Oh dear, whatever will Lori say?" Beth sounded panicked.

"Exactly," Mae said. "Now you're getting my point."

"Does she know?"

"I haven't spoken to her about it," Mae said, "but I've been watching her. I think she knows and she doesn't like it."

Lori's legs buckled and her back slid down the wall. She crouched, arms around her legs, head on her knees, her jeans growing damp from silent tears.

"Paddy, we have to fix this." Beth sounded close to tears again. "This silly feud between them must end. That was the whole purpose of this holiday, and look, we're ten days into their visit and no further forward at all. Things are just getting worse."

"Please don't upset yourself and ruin the day, Bethy," Paddy said. "We'll talk about doing whatever it is Mae suggested, if you think it'll help."

"Good idea, Dad. Let me know if there's anything I can do. More coffee anyone?" Becky said abruptly. "No? Okay, well I guess I'll go and attack the mess in the kitchen."

Alarmed that they would discover her eavesdropping, Lori made a tip-toe dash for the kitchen. Should she quickly start doing the dishes? No, she didn't want to talk to anyone, not just yet, so she ran out the back door and headed for the chicken coop. With shaky hands, she pulled her phone out of her back pocket and dialed Yoni.

"Come on, Yoni, come on," she whispered, willing her husband to answer her call. She turned to look back towards the house and saw Beth, Becky and Aunt Mae standing at the kitchen window, watching her. She waved and smiled, pointed at the phone and turned away. Hopefully, they'd think she was talking to her family and leave her alone.

Yoni had answered but was too busy to talk so had rung off with promises to call her that evening. She didn't repocket the phone but continued to hold it to her ear, in case anyone was still watching her. She watched Becky's pretty little bantam hens scratch the dirt and strut around until she felt composed enough to go back into the house.

By the time everyone else returned from the dam, the kitchen was clean and tidy, and tea and Beth's chocolate cake were ready and waiting on the verandah. Lori did her best to enter into the conversation and feigned interest in the stories of Jake's antics at the dam. Despite her efforts, she caught Becky looking quizzically at her and flashed her what she hoped was a reassuring smile. When Joe and Becky invited her, along with Jake and Carla, to stay for supper, Lori was quick to plead off, blaming the headache she'd claimed earlier.

Becky followed her into the kitchen where she'd gone to collect the quiche dish to take home. "Are you alright sweetie?" she asked.

"Yes, I'm okay, thanks. It's just a headache."

"When you came back from the bike-track, were you out by the chickens all the time? Why didn't you come find us?"

"Yoni called as I was walking back. He wanted to chat." Lori scratched an imaginary spot on the base of the dish, afraid that Becky would see the lie in her eyes.

Becky hugged her close. "Okay, if you say so. But you know I'm here for you, don't you?"

"Yes, of course I know," Lori said, squeezing her eyelids against the tears that had started to prick again. "See you tomorrow, Sis."

Half an hour later, as Paddy swung his carload of three silent passengers off onto the long red road leading home, the setting sun bathed the tree tops with liquid gold in the day's final, glorious hallelujah chorus.

And then it was gone and twilight snuck in.

Chapter 11

Becky contemplated the events and conversations of the day as she closed doors and drew curtains against the chill of evening. The men and boys had disappeared into the den to play Ben's latest football video game, so she went to join Carla in the kitchen.

"Yum, that soup's smelling delicious," Becky said.

"Come taste," Carla said, holding a spoonful of steaming liquid out to Becky.

"Ow, hot but perfect," Becky said. "I'll make a salad and that'll be plenty with leftovers from lunch, won't it?" Slicing tomatoes, she tried to sound nonchalant as she added, "I see you and Jake are very cozy."

Presently, when there was no reply, she looked up. Carla was beaming at her, her eyes sparkling in a way Becky had never seen. She was flushed, apparently not only with the heat of the stove, and brushed a wisp of hair away from her face with the back of her hand. Becky hadn't expected this reaction from her sister.

"Carla," she giggled. "So, it's true."

"Yes, it's true," Carla whispered, quickly shutting the kitchen door.

"But you've always said you didn't want to go out with Jake. What changed your mind?"

"I've always had the hugest crush on him, ever since I was a kid—you know that—and he was always very sweet to me." Carla paused, studying the simmering soup she was stirring. "On my last couple of visits here, he made it very obvious he didn't want to be just friends anymore. But the first time I was still studying, and the second time I'd just started working. It always seemed like bad timing. I don't know; I guess I just wasn't ready to commit."

"So, all this time he's been waiting for you, breaking hearts left, right, and center," Becky said and grinned at Carla. "Joe and I guessed that. But you're such a dark horse. Why didn't you tell me what you were feeling?"

"I don't know," Carla said again. "I certainly didn't lead him on. I didn't tell him *not* to go out with anyone else, so it's not my fault if he's left a string of disappointed would-be girlfriends."

"No, I'm only joking," Becky said. "It's just that no one could understand why he was never interested in any of the girls around here, especially because there are plenty who're interested in him." She flipped the tomato slices into the bowl of lettuce. "I think that's really romantic, him loving you all these years. But just so I understand, now you think you *are* ready to commit?"

"Hmm, yes," Carla said pensively. "I guess I am. It's right, somehow, now, this time." She turned back to the stove. "Soup's ready, Becks. Should I pour it into here?"

"Yes, please," Becky said, chopping cucumber. "What about your job?"

"Ja, well, that's the crunch. I'm dreading speaking to Max about it, but I'll give him proper notice and everything. Hard to believe but just a couple of weeks ago I was arguing with Max about taking a few weeks' holiday, and now here I am, happily thinking of leaving altogether."

She topped the tureen of steaming soup with its lid and turned to Becky, her brow creased with sudden doubt.

"Am I being a fool? How could this have happened so quickly? It's not as if Jake and I have talked about plans or details, it's just like . . . like . . . we sort of *know*."

"Of course you know," Becky said. "This isn't something new. It's been bubbling along under the surface for years. You're not being a fool at all. I'd say you've come to your senses at long last. Jake's a mega catch, and he's already like part of the family."

Carla covered her face with her hands. "One minute I'm feeling absolutely sure and ecstatic, and the next I'm freaking out, scared witless and full of doubts."

"Stop fighting it, Carla," Becky said. "Let yourself be in love with him."

Carla beamed at her again. "Ja, that's it, isn't it? I just have to let my heart win this argument, for once, don't I?"

She came around the kitchen table and gave Becky a spontaneous hug. "Thanks, Sis. It's so great to be able to talk to someone about it. I've been going stir-crazy at home."

"Why? Why aren't you being open about it?"

"Well, for one thing, Lori's going to be furious. She'll hate me even more than she does, if that's possible."

"She doesn't hate you Carla."

"You could have fooled me. You should've seen how she spoke to me at Jake's yesterday afternoon."

"But you're both awful to each other. Don't look at me like that. You're as bad as she is. And I wish you'd both stop, because you're really hurting Mum and Dad. And me."

"You're not there to see her, Becks. It's as if she can't stand to be in the same room as me."

They were silent for a couple of minutes, and suddenly the humming of the fridge and the ticking of the kitchen clock on the wall seemed terribly loud.

"It's always been this way, ever since Tom died, as if she blames me in some way, although I can't think why." Carla wiped her eyes with the kitchen towel she'd been twisting in her hands.

Becky hadn't seen her little sister cry since they were children. "No, no, she doesn't blame you, darling. That's rubbish. I think your meanness to each other has become a horrid habit. You both need to get over yourselves, say you're sorry and give each other a big hug. In fact, I think I'm going to force you both to do that."

Carla laughed. "You never could stand our fighting. It used to make you cry."

Becky gently took Carla's face in her hands. "It still does. So, I'm begging you, *please* sweetie, make peace."

Carla dropped her gaze.

"Lori's no fool," Becky continued, hoping she wasn't going too far. But she had to say it. "I'm sure she's figured it out—you and Jake—and she's scared, which is probably making matters worse."

"Scared? Why?"

"Because she's had two best friends in her life . . . and she lost Tom."

"We all lost Tom," Carla said sharply, but Becky persevered.

"She lost Tom and she's terrified of losing Jake. That's what I think."

Carla looked puzzled. "Why would she lose Jake?"

"Because, you ninny," Becky said, "if you two are hardly on speaking terms, and you go and marry Jake, then she thinks she'll lose him too. In her mind, he'll have made his choice."

Carla was silent for a while. "Have you been talking to her? Tell me the truth, Becks."

"No, I haven't, not about that. But she doesn't have to be a genius to figure it out."

"Who else knows?"

"About you and Jake? Aunt Mae. She spotted it her first day here, I think, the old fox. But Mum and Dad have been seriously slow on the uptake."

Carla covered her face with her hands again and groaned. "You were all gossiping about us today, weren't you? When we went to the dam."

"Of course we were," Becky said and laughed. "You've been found out, so you might as well stop snooping around and start behaving like a real couple."

The kitchen door flew open. It was Joe. "Are we going to starve tonight?" His expression changed as if he instantly understood the scene in the kitchen. Winking at Becky, he added mischievously, "That's no way to treat your man, Carla."

"Cheeky so-and-so," Carla said as she chucked the kitchen towel at him.

It was close to midnight when they drove back to Kalulu. Carla shared the kitchen conversation with Jake—well, most of it, the good bits, not the parts about Lori. She had swiveled around to better see him as she talked. He was smiling his crooked smile and suddenly she felt as though she would burst. Little by little, he'd chipped away at the wall she'd built so carefully around her heart, and now as she let it crumble and fall, she felt overwhelmed by how crazy in love with him she was.

"So, our big secret's out, at last?" He flashed a cheeky grin at her in the half-darkness of the jeep's cab.

"Are you teasing me, Jake Hamilton?"

"Never, baby, not me," he said with mock seriousness, then laughed. "Just a little."

"We're home. Good-bye. You can go." Carla tried to sound offended, but Jake was out and around by her door before she could jump out.

"Oh no you don't, young lady," he said, still smiling. He lifted her down off the seat and set her gently on her feet, but he didn't let her go. "I've been really patient with you for years, Carla Maguire, so excuse me if I'm now good and ready to shout it from the rooftops."

He gently pulled her close and her senses were filled with the sight and scent of him, intoxicated by the sound of his voice, his sweet breath on her face, and his strong arms around her.

"I'm yours, you're mine," he whispered, his lips against her ear, "and I want everyone to know about it."

"Jake . . ." She made a pathetic effort at protesting but his mouth was on hers, gentle at first, but as her arms went around his neck, her hands in his hair, the passion they'd buried for years exploded into this, their first real kiss.

Some moments later they drew apart and stared at each other with breathless astonishment until the corner of Jake's mouth curled into the smile she so loved. "Well, that was worth waiting for."

Carla giggled and pushed him away. "Good night, Jake Hamilton," she whispered over her shoulder before disappearing through the front door of her parents' home.

Jake leaned against his jeep and gazed up at the full moon. It lit up the night sky, bathing the driveway and garden beyond in glittering silver. He felt deeply, deeply happy. But just a moment later, as he turned the key in the ignition and drove away, he frowned as his thoughts turned to Lori. He had a sinking feeling she wasn't going to like this development, not at all.

For the umpteenth time, he wished Tom was alive. He'd have known how to handle Lori. But most of all, Jake just wanted to tell him how he felt about Carla, and his plans for their future, if that was to be.

Irritated by the way the day had turned out and especially her mother and aunt's supper-time chatter, Lori was relieved when at last Paddy, Beth and Mae called it a day and went to bed. She showered and wrapped herself in her robe. Grabbing a fleece blanket from the linen cupboard, she poured a generous tot of Carla's homecoming gift liqueur and padded out in her slippers to enjoy some alone time on the front verandah.

Legs tucked up underneath her in one of the comfy armchairs, she sipped her drink and let the peace and quiet of the night wash over and soothe her ruffled spirit. By the full moon's bright silver light, she could make out the shapes of all the bushes, trees, shrubs and flowers, as well as the *lapa* and pool area down to the right of the garden.

As she tuned into the seeming silence, it became an orchestra of sound. Wind rustled the tree-tops, surging and ebbing much like the sea back home, Lori thought. The delicate tinkling of the swimming pool's little waterfall was hypnotically constant, while frogs croaked intermittently. An owl hooted, once, twice, followed a little later by the shriek of a lemur. She'd heard that sound a few nights before but had forgotten what it was until Beth had reminded her of the lemurs. She wished she could catch a glimpse of the elusive night creatures.

She took another sip and thought about Yoni and the children. She'd called Yoni again on her return from Becky's earlier that evening, this time catching them all at home and free to chat. It had been so good to hear their voices, but she'd hardly been able to hide her disappointment when Yoni told her they wouldn't be flying out to join her. There was a minor crisis on the farm that needed his ongoing supervision, Jonathan was tied up with the pre-army tryouts, and Noya didn't want to travel out on her own. They were all so sorry to be letting her and Beth down, but it just wasn't meant to be. Not this time.

Lori had tried to be upbeat, not wanting to make them feel guiltier than they already did. But she missed them. She would have loved to have them sitting with her there on the verandah, sharing the magic of a moonlit African garden. Beyond that, she desperately needed Yoni's support and level-headed input regarding Carla and Jake.

Her thoughts were interrupted by the sound of an approaching diesel vehicle, followed by the crunch of wheels on the driveway gravel. She didn't hear the bang of car doors closing so, despite her better judgment, she carefully set her glass on the table beside her, pushed the blanket aside, and tip-toed to the edge of the verandah from where she could peep around the corner of the house.

Her eyes widened as she took in the driveway scene. For the second time that day, her legs seemed frozen to the spot as she watched Jake lift Carla down from the car. He was still holding her, and they were talking but Lori couldn't hear what they were saying. And then they kissed.

Lori jerked her head back into the shadows and closed her eyes. Their cinematic embrace hit her like a physical blow. She wished she hadn't seen it, not only because she was ashamed of her spying, but because now there was no denying it. Beth, Becky, and Aunt Mae had been right. They weren't exaggerating at all. In fact, if the moonlit scene was anything to go by, they'd probably grossly underestimated the whole thing.

Lori tiptoed back into the lounge and tried to close and lock the verandah doors as quietly as she could. Hearing the front door open and close and Carla's steps on the flagstone floor of the entrance hall, she bolted across the dark lounge, down the corridor, and into her bedroom, hardly breathing as she quietly clicked her door shut.

Exhausted by the private sea of emotions that had raged within her all day, she climbed under the protective swathes of mosquito netting, slipped between the cool sheets, and fell quickly into the oblivion of a deep sleep.

Chapter 12

Lori awoke but didn't move. Sunday morning. She wondered if it was late. She stretched her hand out to the bedside table beyond the netting and tapped her phone to life. Eight o'clock. She groaned and sat up, rubbing her eyes. Breakfast would be in half an hour.

There was a knocking and then Paddy's voice from the other side of her door.

"Come on lazy bones, the day's half gone."

"Okay, Dad, I'm up." Lori smiled with a strong feeling of déjà vu.

Yet another morning she hadn't gone out for a run, she thought, as she pulled on her robe, clasped her hair away from her face and headed for the bathroom. "Not good," she muttered to herself. Perhaps she'd have time later in the day. And then with a puff of annoyance, she realized there wouldn't be. She'd forgotten; they would all be going to the picnic at one of the local dams after church. She should be helping her mother prepare, she thought guiltily, and hurriedly washed and dressed.

She needn't have worried as everything was under control in the kitchen; two cold boxes and a large wicker hamper were already bulging with everything they could possibly need for a picnic.

"Enough for an army, as usual, my darling," Paddy said as he carried one of the boxes out to the car.

"I'm taking things for Becky, Joe and the boys, as well," Beth said, "and for Jake too, if he wants. I'd rather have too much than too little, Paddy Maguire. It never goes to waste; you know that."

By nine o'clock sharp, the Maguires and Aunt Mae were packed into the car and heading up the road. The drive to the church, located in the center of the large farming area, was nearly an hour long, and they were taking the scenic bush route this morning. The wind had suddenly picked up in the early hours, blowing in a heavy grey cloud cover. It drizzled for part of the way, and they wondered if they'd end up having their packed lunch back at home. Beth had insisted Mae take the front seat for the long drive. She and Mae were in good spirits; they'd enjoyed their work in the kitchen that morning and now continued to chat and laugh.

Lori caught sight of Paddy smiling in the rearview mirror. She knew he loved seeing Beth happy like this, hearing her laugh. Lori felt a sad twinge of jealousy. She envied her mother's even-tempered and loving relationship with her sister. They were so completely on the same wavelength, no hidden meanings, jibes, or jealousies between them. They simply enjoyed each other's company and could spend hours together talking and laughing. She wondered if she and Carla could ever be like that, and then surprised herself by realizing she wished they could.

Lori turned to look out the window at the dirt road—hard and corrugated in some stretches, white with thick sand in others—and the bush beyond. The state of the road didn't allow for fast driving, giving her plenty of time to enjoy the banks of wild flowers and bush trees, their leaves dripping with the recent light rain. She loved these roads and often found herself thinking about them when she was navigating rush-hour traffic back home. But suddenly, her attention was dragged back to the interior of the car.

"Carla," Beth was saying, "is Jake coming today?"

"Oh, yes . . . um, I suppose so," Carla muttered, looking a little flustered.

There was a time, Lori thought as she turned back to the window, that her mother would have asked *her* that question, not Carla. Her mind drifted back to the events of the previous day and her decision on the evening drive home that she'd just have to get used to the idea of what was surely the most questionable match of the century—*if* it really was a match. Perhaps they were all just jumping ahead of themselves, she'd thought, exaggerating the significance of a few glances and the fact that the suspected couple had stayed together for supper with Becky and Joe. But then, what she'd seen later that night in the moonlit driveway had forced her to face up to the facts.

Now, on the long drive to church, a tiny pinprick of an idea suddenly winked in her mind like a firefly in the dark. Maybe, just maybe, the relationship could help make things *better* between her and Carla, rather than worse. But . . . no, surely that was highly unlikely. Wasn't it?

"Good grief, what's wrong with you girls today?" Beth sounded irritated.

"What? Why?" The strange new idea evaporated as Lori turned her attention back to her mother.

"I was asking," Beth said with exaggerated slowness, "if you'd heard from Yoni as to when he and the children will be coming."

"Oh, sorry," Lori replied. "I thought I'd told you. I spoke to them last night, and it doesn't look as though they'll be coming after all."

"Oh, no, I'm so sorry, darling. That's very disappointing for you, and for us. How sad."

"Yes, I was gutted," Lori said. "But there's nothing to do about it. Maybe next time."

"How's Jonathan doing with his try-outs?" Paddy glanced at Lori in the rearview mirror.

"He thinks that what he's done so far went well. He's got another couple of options so he's doing a lot of fitness training. He'll only hear from his first choices in a week or two as to whether or not he made the grade, but he's not too worried. Thanks for asking, Dad."

"What do you feel about him going into the army, dear?" Aunt Mae asked, swiveling in her seat to look at Lori. "It must be difficult for you."

"It is," Lori said frankly. "I didn't grow up with that reality, so it's really hard. But Jonathan wouldn't have it any other way. He feels strongly it's his duty to do his bit towards defending his country, and so on. But it's a big thing, you know. They're just barely out of school, these kids, when they have to deal with some scary situations, even wars."

"Must be tough," Aunt Mae said.

Lori nodded. "I know I'll cry like a baby when he goes in and will no doubt have sleepless nights, but I'm also very aware I can't live in fear. I had a kind of ah-ha moment about that last year."

"You're right," Paddy said as he slowed down to steer the car over a particularly rocky patch of the road. "The Bible is very clear about God actually *commanding* us not to fear. It's an important and often-repeated command."

Lori caught sight of Carla shaking her head, and stiffened. "Do you have something to say, Carla?"

Carla turned a steely stare onto her. "No, nothing at all," she answered coolly.

Beth put her arm around Lori's shoulders and pulled her close, kissing her on the temple. "I'm sorry, darling, that you have to deal with all this," she said. "You've been so quiet and withdrawn these last couple of days, and you look so sad sometimes, I can't bear it for you. Your Dad and I are praying for you, sweetheart."

"Thanks Mum, he'll be fine." But she had an inkling that Beth wasn't only talking about Jonathan's upcoming army service.

"Just to warn you, Lori," Paddy said as he turned into the parking lot of the local club, "Robert, the English bloke we told you about a few days ago, comes from a background of replacement theology. Not sure where he stands now, but just wanted to let you know in case it came up."

"Okay, thanks for the heads-up. But I really don't know if I'll be up to having any serious conversation today."

"You'll have to try not to get on your high-horse about Israel and embarrass Mum and Dad," Carla said pointedly.

"Seriously Carla?" Lori gritted her teeth and tried to control her instant annoyance. "Just . . . don't!"

"Girls, girls, please," Beth said. "Let's try and enjoy the day together, for goodness' sake."

"So, just keep her away from me," Lori muttered as she jumped out the car and pasted on a smile as someone came forward to greet them. How had she imagined, even for a split second, that they could ever reconcile, especially through Jake?

The farm block's communal club was used by all the farmers living in the area for every kind of event from business meetings to parties and even horse-riding competitions. 'Church' was a plain, high-ceilinged rectangular building nestled in a corner of the club grounds. Lori tried to compose herself as she followed Paddy to their seats in the row behind Becky, Joe, and the boys.

On this particular Sunday morning, the church was about half full. Lori looked around her, smiling at some familiar faces. On the final note of the first hymn, sung lustily by the motley gathering of men, women, and children to the accompaniment of an old piano and three guitars, Jake arrived. Lori was surprised to see him stride down the aisle to take the empty seat at Carla's side. Normally, he would have slipped unobtrusively into an empty chair in the back row.

Lori frowned as Jake took Carla's hand before nodding his greeting to the rest of the family. She glanced at her parents, noticing that they looked like two cats who'd stolen the cream. She shook her head, took a deep breath and tried to focus on the farmer-cum-preacher who was now standing on the slightly raised platform.

An hour later, the final blessing was given. As people turned in their chairs to chat with each other, Lori escaped outside. The morning clouds had broken up to reveal large patches of deep blue sky, and the sun was very warm. Perfect weather for a picnic, after all.

Chapter 13

"So, you live in Israel."

Lori smiled up at the pleasant-faced man to whom she'd been introduced earlier that day.

"Yes, Hugh, I do. For many years now," she said.

Lori and Hugh's wife, Rose, had been given the task of buttering a mountain of bread rolls. They were working at one of three long tables placed under a clump of tall trees by a large dam. The other picnickers were busy unpacking the contents of their hampers and cold boxes onto the remaining tables while trying to keep an eye on the excited antics of the smaller children. The coals in three portable barbecues were being fanned into a red-hot glow and would soon be sizzling in the juices of fat steaks and coils of *boerewors*, the spicy hand-made sausage popular throughout southern Africa.

Rose handed her husband a knife. "You can butter while you talk, honey," she said with a smile.

"I went there once, ages ago," Hugh said, acquiescently putting his drink down and picking up a roll. "Absolutely loved it."

"Did you volunteer on a kibbutz?" Lori asked.

"No, no. A friend and I traveled there for a few weeks when we finished agricultural college. I'd always been fascinated by the idea of Jerusalem and wanted to see it for myself. Man, I wasn't disappointed. I've wanted to take Rose there, but we haven't managed it yet. It's on our bucket list though, isn't it, hon? Once the kids have flown the nest."

Before Rose could answer, a younger man who had been standing by stepped closer.

"I'm not too sure what to think about Israel," he said.

Lori glanced up at him as she added a buttered roll to the pile. "I don't think we've met before," she said, although she had a pretty good idea of who he was.

"I'm Robert, Jack Tanner's manager."

"New here?" Lori asked, thinking he had a nice smile.

"If you call a year and a half new, then yes, I suppose I'd be the new boy on the block."

Lori laughed. "Guess it's been a while since my last visit here." She held out her hand. "I'm Lori, Paddy and Beth Maguire's daughter."

Robert returned her firm hand-shake.

"Easy to spot the Maguire connection," he said.

Lori looked up at him questioningly and Robert gestured toward his own face with the bottle he was holding. "You've got your Dad's eyes."

"The Maguire give-away," Rose said.

"Why do you say you're not sure about Israel?" Lori asked.

"Well," Robert said, pulling up a camp-chair, "I'm from the U.K. as you can probably hear."

Lori nodded. His English accent was unmistakable.

"And I grew up in a church there that holds the view that Israel is no longer of any specific relevance from a spiritual point of view."

"Replacement theology," Lori said flatly.

"What's that?" Rose asked.

Robert took a swig of his drink and paused as if carefully considering his answer before speaking. "Hmm, I wouldn't call it that, exactly."

"So, what would you call it?" Her roll-buttering work done, Lori wiped her hands on a paper napkin and leaned back in her chair, primed for any kind of debate this young man cared to have.

"The pastor in my church in England supported covenant or reformed theology. There's a difference—I can try and explain if you want," Robert said.

Lori nodded encouragingly so he continued.

"Replacement theology is basically the belief that the church has replaced Israel in God's plan, meaning that the Jews are no longer God's 'chosen race', and that God doesn't have any specific plans for the future of the nation of Israel. Also, that God's promises to Israel that we read in the Bible are now relevant for the Church, rather than for Israel."

A few other picnickers had gathered around to listen. Robert cleared his throat and ploughed on. "In short, they believe that the Jews, or Israelites as they were called in the Old Testament, had their chance and blew it."

"Wow. That's harsh," said Hugh. "And the other theologies?"

"They don't say that the church has *replaced* Israel," Robert said.

Paddy had also been listening as he made himself a steak sandwich. Plate in hand, he drew up a camp-chair next to Lori who smiled at him before turning her attention back to Robert.

"So, what *do* they say?" she asked, interested to hear how he would clarify it.

"That there's one people of God who may be both Jewish and Gentile."

"Ag, I don't understand," Rose said, throwing her hands up.

"It's based on faith, not race," Robert said. "Think of it like a tree. The Israelites were the olive tree but then God *pruned* unbelieving Jews from the tree and *grafted in* believing and faithful Gentiles. So, nobody's being replaced; it's more like two becoming one. One people of Jews *and* Gentiles who are all saved by grace through faith and their belief."

Lori stood up to fetch herself something to eat. "Do you believe that the Jewish people no longer have any special relevance to God?" she asked. "But before you answer, can I get you a plate of food? We'll keep you talking until everything's finished if you're not careful."

"I'll come help myself, thanks," Robert said, joining her at the table. "Do I believe it?" he repeated while selecting a coil of *boerewors*. "I'm not sure."

Lori settled herself back in her chair, her plate balanced on her knees and smiled up at Robert.

"I don't," she said simply.

Robert seemed a bit taken aback by her forthrightness. "Okay . . ."

"I'm afraid I'm not a great biblical scholar or theologian," Lori said, "but I was raised to take the Bible at face-value. So, when the Bible says that God is the same yesterday, today and forever, I believe it. And when it says that God is not a liar that He should change His mind, I believe that too."

"That's my standing," Hugh agreed. "If God made a covenant with Abraham and promises to Isaac, Jacob, King David, and a whole bunch of others, then I believe those covenants and promises stand. They're not going to disappear because God has changed His mind about the Israelites."

"But He did get mad with them sometimes," Rose said turning to Paddy, "didn't He?"

"Yes, He did," Paddy said. "But the Bible is full of references as to how God continues to love and forgive the Jewish people. Isaiah talks about how God can never forget Israel, and the prophet Jeremiah says that the Jewish people will exist as a nation forever."

"To me," Lori said, "one of the greatest witnesses to God's everlasting faithfulness to the nation of Israel is the existence of the Jewish people today. It's totally miraculous if you look at all the ghastly attempts down through history to wipe them off the face of the earth. Not only have they survived, but the modern state of Israel is prospering. In fact, it's been dubbed 'the start-up nation' because it's been the birthplace of so many amazing inventions, and what's more, many of the world's biggest corporations are doing business there."

"Oh, ja, I read about that," Hugh said. "Incredible."

Lori looked around the circle of mostly silent listeners. She suddenly became aware of the high-pitched voices of children at play, the chatter of those watching over them or the still-burning *braais*, a woman's shriek and then guffaws of laughter from down by the water.

Paddy nodded pensively. "I do agree with the Apostle Paul when he says the Jewish people are a great example of God's unending grace," he said eventually. "In *spite* of their history of rebellion, Paul teaches in the New Testament that God still loves and preserves and protects them. And I think there's good evidence of that to this day."

Carla, Jake and a couple of other young farmers, wet from swimming in the dam, sauntered up to the table and helped themselves to food.

"You're all looking very serious," Jake said as he piled a couple of steaks onto his plate. "What have we missed?"

"We've been talking about Israel and whether or not God's promises are still meant for them," Rose said.

"What d'you think, Jake?" Hugh asked.

Jake pulled up a couple of camp chairs and motioned to Carla to sit down next to him. Grinning, he waved his fork in Lori's general direction. "Whatever *she* says!"

"Chicken," Lori said, smiling at Jake before turning back to the initiator of the whole discussion.

"You should really come to Israel, Robert, to see it for yourself."

"Ja," Hugh said. "You should, man. It's got its own special kind of magic that draws you in."

"You'll learn lots and I think you'll probably discover that not everything is as it seems or what the media would have you believe," Lori said.

"What do *you* think about Israel, Carla?" Robert asked suddenly.

Lori glanced over at Carla who seemed surprised by Robert's question, and a little uncomfortable.

"Well . . ." she said slowly, pushing her food around her plate.

"You must have seen a different side of the country, being able to see it with Lori and not just as a tourist," Hugh said.

"Oh no," Lori said, shaking her head. "Carla's never even been to Israel."

"What? Why?" Hugh asked.

"I . . . I guess I just never had the opportunity," Carla said, her cheeks flushing red.

"Oh, come on, Carla," Lori said, her tone like dry ice. "You've had plenty of opportunity. You've just never wanted to come."

"Really? Why ever not?" Hugh blurted before being elbowed into silence by his wife.

Carla swallowed, laid down her knife and fork and lifted her chin. "I don't agree with their politics and I don't want to support an apartheid state in any way."

Lori was stunned. She'd heard Carla make snide remarks about Israel in the past, but she'd never realized the extent of her hostility. This was the country that she called home that Carla was talking about, the land where her children had been born. How could her own sister have the gall to say something like that, and especially here, in front of everyone?

Carla kept her eyes fixed on Robert who seemed intent on continuing the conversation. "When I was in London last year," he said, "I saw quite a few banners and demonstrations against the 'apartheid state of Israel'."

"I've seen posts about it on social media a few times," Rose said, "but I've heard from friends who've been there that it's not exactly what you'd call an apartheid state. And those of us who grew up in South Africa would know what that is, hey?"

"It's that kind of propaganda that makes me really mad and sad at the same time," Lori said. "So many people are willing to listen and buy into it without questioning or even bothering to try and find out the truth. Most of them have probably never even been there to see for themselves if it's true or not—like my sister, for example." She cast a withering glance in Carla's direction. "It totally baffles me how intelligent people who should surely know better simply accept this stuff because someone else says it's so."

"On what authority do you say it's *not* an apartheid state?" Carla said, her voice rising.

Lori's eyes narrowed as she looked across at her sister. She knew Carla was pushing her on purpose but, furious and deeply hurt, she couldn't help but respond.

"On what authority?" Lori repeated deliberately. "Well, let's think." She couldn't keep the sarcasm out of her voice. "I guess because I've lived there for the last twenty-odd years, for starters. Also, because when I gave birth to my kids, the women lying in the beds on either side of me were Arab. My dentist is a dear Arab man, and every time I'm at a hospital I can't help noticing that the majority of nurses, doctors and patients are Arab. Because when you get on a bus or a train, you'll probably be sitting next to an Arab person. When you go to the toilet in a shopping mall, you can smile at the Arab woman washing her hands at the basin next to you. Because the major universities all over Israel are full of Arab students who are free to study or demonstrate or do whatever they please, just like university students all over the world. Oh yes, and you'll be amazed at the queues of Jewish Israelis waiting to eat at one of the famous Arab humous restaurants or kiosks. Hmm, what else? One of my good friends and fellow teachers is an Arab lady; Yoni and I went to her beautiful daughter's wedding a couple of months ago. Oh, and let's not forget the Arab members of the Knesset—you know, the Israeli Parliament—who are democratically voted into their positions." She paused and looked directly at Carla. "I guess *those* are just some of the reasons why I think the label 'apartheid state' doesn't apply to Israel."

There was a short silence as everyone stared at her, wide-eyed.

"Well that certainly doesn't sound like apartheid to me," one of Jake's friends said.

Carla laid her almost untouched plate of food on the table behind her. "One man's freedom can be another man's apartheid," she murmured.

Lori chose to ignore the remark. "I'm not saying Israel is right about everything. It's not. Believe me, there's a lot I think is wrong or would change if I could. It's an incredibly complex situation that can't be understood in a five-minute discussion or wrapped up in a neat little box. But there are people there, of all races and religions, who are working together towards a better, more peaceful future for everyone. Let me ask you this: how many churches and Christians obey God's order to pray for the peace of Jerusalem? Or is it just easier to criticize and believe the worst, without bothering to find out for yourself?"

Lori felt the blood pumping in her cheeks as she glared around the group of people, some who stared back at her with raised eyebrows and others who looked away uncomfortably. She didn't dare look at Paddy.

"Grandpa." Riley's voice broke the awkward silence. "Will you come play volley ball with us, Grandpa, pleeeze?"

Carla jumped up. "I'll come, Riley. I've been lectured enough for one afternoon."

But Riley stood his ground. "Come on Grandpa. Granny says *you* must come and play."

Lori thought Paddy looked relieved as he grinned at his grandson. "We must always do what Granny says, mustn't we? Come on, pull your old Grandpa up."

Riley pulled and Paddy rose from his chair with make-believe groans.

"Well, friends," he said. "We can talk and discuss and debate, and that's a good thing, but we're not going to solve the world's problems in one sitting, especially not where Israel's concerned. It's a big subject that

I think is worthy of our careful contemplation and daily prayers, and I'd say we've been given a lot of food for thought. Now, who's for a game of volleyball before tea?"

Following his cue, most of the group dispersed, some to join in the game, others to wander down to the water's edge. Only Robert, Jake and Lori remained sitting.

"I'm sorry," Robert said. "Perhaps I shouldn't have raised the subject."

Lori shook her head and waved her hand in dismissal. "It's okay."

"I think I'll try do that sometime soon, though . . . visit Israel, I mean," Robert said. "I'd like to see it for myself."

"You'll love it," Lori said. "And be sure to let us know when you come over. We'd be happy to have you for a meal or even to stay. My husband, Yoni, is always ready for a good debate," she added, trying to muster a smile.

"You really should go, Rob," Jake said as he stood up. "It's a seriously cool place, and you needn't worry, Yoni's not nearly as scary as she is."

Lori laughed as Jake and Robert walked away, but she really felt like crying. She hadn't been able to resist Carla's challenge and as a result had been sucked into a public display, no doubt disappointing her father . . . and Jake. She felt awful, but it was too late. There was nothing she could do about it now.

Chapter 14

Lori noticed Jake signaling to her from the water's edge, waving her down to the dam and pointing at one of the double kayaks. She shook her head in refusal, but he didn't give up that easily.

"Come on, Lori, get down here," he called. "We're going out for a row, and I won't take no for an answer."

Lori relented and walked down to the water's edge. She clambered into the kayak while Jake held it steady. He handed her an oar, climbed in behind her and they were off, their oars dipping in and out of the water in perfect unison as if it was just yesterday that they'd taken a kayak out together. Lori loved rowing and felt the tension flowing out of her body with each slap of oar on water.

"Haven't lost your touch, Titch," Jake said at last.

Lori grinned without looking back. She rested the oar over her knees while she soaked up the scene before her. The winds had disappeared hours earlier so the water was glass-still, mirroring the white clouds in the blue sky above.

"Fish eagle," Jake said.

Lori looked in the direction he was pointing and was delighted to see the big bird sitting still and majestic on the tallest of the waterlogged trees in the middle of the dam.

"Ah, how beautiful. I wonder if it has a mate."

"Yeah," Jake said. "Apparently there's a pair nesting around here but we didn't see them when we were out earlier."

"You were probably making too much noise," she said. "I'm so glad they're a pair; that's great."

Suddenly, the eagle spread its wings and launched itself into the air with a single, haunting cry. It sailed the wind to the far end of the dam and disappeared into the trees.

"The sound of Africa," Lori said softly. "Gives me goose-bumps."

"Always reminds me of Tom," Jake said.

"Me too. He loved them. They were his favorite type of bird." She paused. "I see them in my dreams sometimes, fish eagles, or more accurately, one eagle."

They were silent for a while and Lori let Jake steer them down toward the end of the dam across water sparkling silver and gold as the sun dropped lower in the sky. She instinctively knew what was coming so wasn't surprised when Jake spoke.

"He wouldn't be happy with what's going on, Titch."

It still hurt to hear it out loud and tears stung her eyes for the second time that afternoon. She stared straight ahead and didn't answer.

"What is it with you two?" Jake asked.

"I don't know," Lori said hesitantly. "She just pushes all my buttons."

"Why?"

"She's a spoilt brat, for starters."

"She's not, Lor, she's really not. *Damn*, you're hard on her."

"You sound like Becky."

"Well, maybe it's about time you listen to us."

"Jake Hamilton," Lori said, turning an attempt at a smile over her shoulder in an effort to lighten the mood. "I do believe you're somewhat biased."

"No, I don't think I am. I've known you both forever. And I think I can say that you and I know each other better than anyone else."

"Yes, but that doesn't mean you know Carla. The *real* Carla. She hasn't lived here for years."

"I do know her, Lori." Jake sounded exasperated. "I've gotten to know her very well over the last few years when you haven't been around. She's a great person. She's not perfect, but then neither am I—or you, for that matter. You've probably figured out that I'm crazy about her; that's a no-brainer, especially for you. What I can't understand is why my very best friend, the person who sees inside my head and who's always been there for me, even from across the other side of the world, can't make peace with the woman I love. Especially when she's her own sister."

Lori didn't answer. She wasn't blind. She did know him better than anyone else and if she was brutally honest with herself, she'd suspected that Carla had captured his heart as soon as she'd noticed him glancing at her in the rear-view mirror on the way home from the airport the day of their arrival. And then there were all the other flirtations, looks and brushing touches, not to mention the midnight kiss. But to hear him say it now, so matter-of-factly, made her throat tighten and her eyes sting. She couldn't respond, even if she'd wanted to.

Yet again, she tried to analyze her feelings. Was she jealous? I can't be, she decided once again. That wouldn't be fair. I've been married for years. How can I deny Jake the same happiness? He must have been lonely all these years. He'd make the most wonderful husband and any kid would be lucky to have him as a father. No, I'm not jealous, she concluded. So, what? Why did the idea of Jake and Carla make her stomach knot and churn with nausea?

"Lor?"

"Why Carla, Jake? Why *her*?"

"Why Carla? Well, in case you hadn't noticed, she's drop-dead gorgeous. You Maguire women have cornered the market on looks in these parts but, no offence, *she* is the most beautiful woman I've ever seen. I know that it sounds like a cliché but she takes my breath away sometimes when I look at her."

Lori could hear the smile in his voice. "That's not enough for a relationship," she said sharply.

"No, it's not. So luckily, she's also a great person, as I've already said. She's funny and sweet and kind and generous. She has a great sense of humor, she's faithful and loyal. She's very intelligent . . ."

"Sounds like *someone's* seeing her through rose-colored spectacles," Lori said sarcastically.

"No, I'm not, not at all. Like you, she can be a stubborn pain in the neck sometimes. And this whole thing with you is getting on my nerves. I can't handle it anymore. I thought I could make it right, but now I'm not so sure. No one can do that except you two. Please, Lor, *please*, do that. For me."

"Do what?" Lori asked. She wasn't going to make this easy for him.

"Be the adult and make it right between you and Carla."

She shook her head. "Don't know if I can, Jake."

"You can. If anyone can do it, you can." He paused and stopped rowing. "If you want to, of course. And I'm asking, no, I'm *begging* you to want to."

"Why? What does it matter to you?" Lori took up the slack and flicked each end of her oar into the water on either side of the kayak, shattering the reflections of cloud.

"It matters," Jake said, now matching her strokes so the kayak sped across the water. "You are a huge and important part of my life. You *know* that."

"But I don't live anywhere near you anymore. We only see each other once every year or two, if we're lucky." Lori made several deep strokes on the right side of the kayak so as to turn it around in the direction of their starting point.

"It doesn't make a difference. I can't be with someone who doesn't accept and love you like I do. You're one of the most important pieces of my life. I'm pretty sure you always will be, and the woman I marry needs to be okay with that."

The tears now dripped unchecked down Lori's face but her back was straight, her shoulders steady as she plunged the oar in and out of the water, grateful for the exertion.

"That's a tall order," she said at last when she was sure her voice would be steady.

"Well, it's a fact. Even though you're a giant pain, as I've already said."

"Might be mission impossible for Carla."

"No, I don't agree, Lor. I'm pretty sure she's just waiting for a break-through. I think she's hating the way things are now and she'll jump at the chance to make it right. Deep down she admires and misses you; she *wants* to respect you, because she still loves you."

"And I think you're living in la-la land, or you don't know her as well as you think you do," Lori said. "She hates my guts, Jake."

"No, she doesn't."

"Grief, who's being the stubborn pain in the neck now?"

"Tom would want you to, Lor," Jake said in a low voice, "to make it right with her. You know he would."

By now, they were close to the bank so she jumped out of the kayak into the shallow water and whirled to face him.

"No, I don't *know* he would," she snarled. "Because he's not here. And stop using him as emotional blackmail against me, Jake. It's beneath you. If you want to be with Carla, then go for it. Like I said, it's got *nothing* to do with me."

She threw her oar on the ground and stormed up the bank, leaving Jake sitting speechless in the kayak.

Finding Paddy having a cup of tea with Beth, Becky, Aunt Mae, and other friends, Lori crouched down beside him, gripping his chair handle to still her shaking hands.

"Can we go home, please Dad?" she whispered. "Or maybe I can take the car? You can all come home with Becky or Jake, whenever you want."

Paddy stared down at Lori.

"Please Dad." She saw his face soften into a look of concern.

"Go start packing up our things, sweetheart," he said. "We'll leave as soon as we can."

Lori ignored the questioning looks from Beth, Aunt Mae, and Becky as she stood up and headed for the car; she wasn't in the mood for explaining anything to anyone.

She heard Paddy speak behind her. "Sorry Becks, but we need to go," was all he said.

A little while later, their belongings were gathered and loaded into the car. Lori did her best to paint on a smile as she said her good-byes to the kind and friendly people with whom they'd spent the day. She could hardly breathe but thought she managed to put on a good show. She knew Becky wasn't fooled though, her eyes questioning as they hugged good-bye.

"I'm sorry, we haven't had a minute together all day," Becky said.

"It's okay." Lori avoided her gaze and tried to keep it together.

"I'll see you tomorrow, okay?"

"Ja, sure," Lori muttered, pulling away.

"Don't you just love this golden evening light?" Becky gestured towards the scene around them. "It's so beautiful. Do you have to go? This is always my best time of day."

"Mosquito hour, Becks," Lori said dully.

"Negative ninny." Becky smiled. "Go on then but be sure to watch the sunset on your way home; it's going to be a stunner."

Lori felt guilty for being so sullen and kissed her sister on the cheek. "Love you lots, Becks. Thanks for always being so sweet. Go home and get some rest."

"No need. I've been terribly lazy all day, waited on hand and foot by Mum and Aunt Mae. Absolute heaven. But you look like you need a good night's sleep."

Lori nodded and climbed into the back seat of the car, not trusting herself to say anything more. The last goodbyes were said and they were off.

"Where's Carla?" Aunt Mae asked as they bumped down the narrow track.

"She'll come home later with Jake," Beth answered.

As the stretch of sandy road between them and the picnickers lengthened, Lori leaned back against the seat and closed her eyes with relief. Aunt Mae reached over and took her hand.

No-one commented on the cinematic sunset blazing across the early evening sky, now in front of them, now to one side as they followed the bends and turns of the bush road. Nor did they react to the children who ran along the side of the road beside them, trailing home-made toy cars of wire behind them. Not a word more was said, all the way home to Kalulu.

Chapter 15

Lori was helping Beth carry trays of steaming soup and buttered toast into the lounge when they heard a jeep draw up outside.

"That'll be Carla and Jake," Beth said. "Do we have enough soup for Jake? I'll go make more toast."

As she turned back towards the kitchen, Carla burst in through the front door. Quickly closing it behind her, she leant against it with her eyes closed, her face flushed and her breathing heavy.

"Where's Jake?" Beth asked. "You're just in time for supper."

Carla lunged away from the door and made her way across the lobby and lounge in a few strides. "He won't be coming in."

Lori and Beth followed her into the lounge and put the trays down as Carla stopped at the doorway to the bedroom wing and glared back at them.

"It's *over*! Are you happy now?" Her voice broke and her face crumpled as the tears began to flow.

"Carla . . ." Lori started, taking a step toward her but Carla held up a shaking finger as she stepped backwards.

"Don't you *ever* speak to me again," she said, her voice trembling and low. "You're just so *jealous* you couldn't stand it," she sobbed. "I *hate* you!" She turned and ran down the passageway to her bedroom.

Paddy, Beth and Aunt Mae all winced as the door slammed and then slowly turned to look at Lori.

"What?" Lori cried. "Do you think *I've* got something to do with this?"

Their silence couldn't hide the looks on their faces, which confirmed that yes, that was exactly what they thought.

"I haven't. I didn't do or say anything. Jake's probably just come to his senses, that's all."

"Lori," Beth said, frowning. "I can't believe you can be so . . . so horrible to each other. Just beastly, and I'm *sick* of it. You should be ashamed of yourself."

Lori stared at her mother in dismay. She'd never heard Beth speak like that to anyone. She was cut to the quick, her despair deepening when Beth began to cry.

"Mum . . ." she started, but Paddy stood up between them.

"I suggest you go to bed, Lori," he said in a quiet voice that frightened her. "Just go, now. Please."

Devastated, Lori left the room, closing the heavy passage door quietly behind her. She was numb, unable even to cry despite her parents' stinging words, and slumped onto her bed, wishing she could forget that today had ever happened.

"Oh dear." Beth dropped onto the couch next to Mae and buried her face in her hands, "I shouldn't have lost my temper. I shouldn't have said those *awful* things. Poor Lori, and poor, poor Carla."

Mae enveloped Beth in a comforting hug. "Don't cry, Bethy darling. They'll be alright, you'll see. Things will work out."

But Beth shook her head. Perhaps there wasn't any hope; perhaps they would just have to accept the horrible status quo.

Paddy slumped back down into his chair. "Have we just gone back in time?"

Mae began to chuckle. "I do believe we have. Teenage temper tantrums at the ripe old ages of 29 and 40."

"Outrageous," Beth said as she dabbed her tears away with a tissue, smiling despite herself. Mae always managed to make her see the funny side of things.

"Hopefully," Paddy said, lifting his supper tray back onto his knees, "it's the storm before the calm."

"We just need to keep on praying and believing. You'll see, they'll come around." Mae spooned jam onto her toast. "They'll be best buddies before your birthday if we just don't give up hope."

"I'm hanging onto my very last thread of hope, as hard as I can," Beth said, "but I'm really beginning to wonder."

"No," Mae said firmly. "You can't give up hope, Bethy."

"I wish we could just leave them here alone, to fight it out," Paddy muttered, almost to himself.

"What? What did you say?" Beth said.

Paddy took a bite of toast and munched as if to give himself time to consider what he'd just blurted out. "Perhaps we should just leave and let them get on with it, fight it out, say everything that's boiling around inside of them until they get it out of their systems."

"Don't be ridiculous, Paddy," Beth responded immediately but then decided, on second thought, that Paddy might be on to something. "How could we do that?"

"I think that's a marvelous idea!" Mae put down her knife. "You brilliant man. *That's* the intervention we talked about at Becky's. We could fly to Lusaka with Joe. He told me today he's going there in a couple of days, taking the boys to visit his parents while he does some business. Quick trip before the baby comes. His plane is big enough for all of us, isn't it?"

"No, no, Mae, don't be silly. We can't leave them alone."

"Come on, Beth. Paddy's probably got business to do in the city, and you and I can do some fun shopping. Things for your party, and you know I always love going to those marvelous curio shops."

"We can't just land on Joe's parents with no proper warning."

"We won't," Mae said matter-of-factly. "We, my dear, will go and stay in a hotel. You told me you stayed in quite a nice one on your last trip there, didn't you?"

Paddy chuckled. "Now you're onto something, Mae."

Mae beamed. "Come on, Beth. It'll be fun. And you can seriously do with a break from all this." She waved her hand in the direction of the bedroom wing.

Beth's worried frown slowly began to relax into a smile. It was tempting. And she *could* do with a break. She was beginning to realize what an exhausting effect the tension between her daughters was having on her.

"Do you really think we can do it, Paddy?" she asked. "Leave them alone? They'll be furious with us."

Paddy grinned. He'd regained his appetite and spread a lavish helping of butter onto a second, thick slice of toast. "I'll speak to Joe about it first thing in the morning," he declared with a firm nod and Beth knew that his mind was made up.

"Come on Bethy, let's have a glass of that liqueur Carla brought with her, to celebrate."

But before Paddy could get up from his armchair to bring the drinks Lori came back into the lounge, surprising her parents and aunt who thought she'd gone to bed already.

"Can I have the car please, Dad?" she asked, pulling on a light jacket.

Paddy's brow furrowed as he looked up at her. "Where're you going? It's late."

"It's not even nine o'clock Dad. Can I take the car please? I won't be long."

"Okay," Paddy said reluctantly, waving his hand in the direction of the lobby. "You know where the keys are. Be careful, please."

"Thanks," she muttered as she headed out the room.

They heard the clinking of keys, the opening and shutting of the front door, and a few seconds later, the sound of Paddy's car reversing out of its parking lot and crunching up the drive.

"Where on earth is she going?" Beth asked. "Paddy, you shouldn't have let her take the car."

"She's not a child, Beth. I didn't have any reason not to let her take it. She'll be fine. Probably gone to chat things over with Becky."

"No, too late for that," Mae said. "I'll bet she's gone to Jake."

"Whatever for?" Beth asked.

"To make peace perhaps? I guess we'll just have to wait and see."

The headlights swept across the lawn and then the brick walls as Lori drove up to Jake's house. She wondered if he'd even let her in. Perhaps he was asleep already, but no, the lights were on. She bit her bottom lip nervously as she walked up the stone steps to his verandah—the very steps she'd run down blindly just a few days before—and knocked on the door.

"Jake?"

No answer.

"Jake? It's Lori. Can we talk pl—"

"I know who it is." An unsmiling Jake pulled the door open, making her jump. "What're you doing here?"

She stared at him. This was worse than she expected. "Can I come in?"

Wordlessly, he stood aside, holding the door open as she passed by and into his lounge.

Lori eyed the plate of half-eaten food on the stool next to his chair. "Sorry to interrupt your supper."

She stood in the middle of the room, her hands shoved deep in her pockets. She'd never felt so uncomfortable in Jake's presence before.

Jake's manners won out and he motioned to her to sit on the couch, clearing a space for her among the papers and files piled there. "Getting ready for my trip to Lusaka tomorrow," he muttered.

Lori perched herself on the very edge of the couch.

"Want anything to eat?"

"No, no thanks. You carry on." She sat in silence, studying her hands in her lap and then looking blankly at the TV until Jake switched it off and looked at her questioningly.

"What're you doing here?" he asked again as he crunched on his last slice of buttered toast.

Lori stopped fiddling and looked directly at him. "Don't do it, Jake."

"Don't do what?"

"Break up with her. I'm saying, don't break up with her. Don't do that," she shook her head for emphasis. "Please don't."

Jake leant back against the worn leather backrest of his chair and scratched his head, a puzzled look on his face. "I thought that's exactly what you wanted me to do."

She shook her head again, twisting the single gold band on her ring finger this way and that, before she dared to look at him again. "You don't have to do everything I want, you know." Her attempt at a joke fell flat as he just kept looking straight at her, his usually kind eyes steely. Her chest hurt and it was suddenly hard to breathe. "Don't hate me, please, Jake," she whispered. "I couldn't bear that."

No response.

"I was scared of losing you to Carla. She hates me, so I thought if you were with her, we couldn't be friends anymore. We couldn't be . . . who we are." She took a deep breath. "But you can't break up with her because of me. You'll end up hating me anyway."

No response.

She sniffed against the back of her hand and tried to blink back stubborn tears. "But you deserve to be happy. And Carla makes you happy, I can see that, and it's good. I want you to be happy, Jake. You deserve to have a family and kids of your own, and all the rest of it. I get it that you've been waiting for her all these years. I never figured it out before, but I know that now. And if that's what you want—and *who* you want—then don't let me mess it up."

There was still no response so she took a deep breath and raised her eyes to look at him. She was taken aback to see he was almost smiling.

"C'mon Jake, don't make me grovel."

"Why? You're doing a good job of it."

She shook her head again. "Don't, Jake. This isn't funny."

"Are you doing this for me or for Carla?"

His question caught her off guard. At first, she thought she knew the answer, but then she wasn't so sure so didn't answer him.

"I'm not going to break up with her, Lori."

He rarely used her full name, only on the most serious occasions. Or when he was mad or disappointed with her. She wasn't sure of the current reason. She wasn't sure of anything.

"You're not? But she said . . . she came back home, all ranting and raving that I'd ruined everything, and that you'd gone . . . and . . ."

"We had an argument and I said I wasn't coming in. I was too mad about how the whole day had gone, and I was really disappointed with the both of you. You behaved like a couple of idiots all day. It was embarrassing, especially for your parents, and I don't like seeing them put on the spot like that. So, I didn't feel like being in the same room with the two of you again today; I'd had enough."

"But that's not so dramatic. Was she just over-reacting, as usual?"

"Stop being catty about her, Lor. You can't even help yourself, can you?"

"Sorry. I'm sorry. Go on." Lori bit her lip to stop herself from talking again.

"I said I didn't want to come in, that I wouldn't see her again for a few days and that we could both do with a bit of space to think."

"Ah . . ."

"I was about to tell her I had to go to Lusaka for a few days' business but she jumped out the car and ran into the house. I thought about going after her to explain. I'd even thought about asking her if she wanted to come with me. But instead I decided I should leave her alone to cool down. Perhaps a few days without seeing each other would give some proportion to everything."

"That's a bit unkind, don't you think? I mean, she really thought it's over."

"Then maybe she was over-reacting a bit. She was very upset by the whole day. You really got under her skin."

"It was mutual, believe me."

"I know. I was there, remember?"

"Well, aren't you going to call her or something?"

"No."

"Bit of a risk, isn't it? What if you come back from Lusaka and she doesn't want anything to do with you?"

"Not going to happen. It's meant to be Lor, so we'll work it out. If only you two could work out whatever it is you have going on."

Lori nodded. "I think the folks have had enough."

"Not surprised. It's really hard to be around."

"I guess that's why we haven't met up for the last I don't know how many years."

"That's just avoiding the issue. Avoiding. Denying. Doesn't fix anything."

Lori nodded slowly.

"You should really be ashamed of yourselves, you two." Jake leant forward earnestly. "You're family, siblings. That's such a gift. Don't take it for granted. I wish I had brothers and sisters. But I don't. You and Tom are the closest damn thing to blood relatives I've ever had, but still it's not the same. Don't throw it away, Lor, your relationship with Carla. She's your sister and deep down, underneath all that prickly self-defense, she loves and admires you. She always has."

"That's what Becky says, but you could've fooled me. She doesn't exactly behave like that, does she?"

"Neither do you, so why should she? One of you has to be the bigger person. Hold out an olive branch, for goodness' sake. You'll see how quickly she'll grab it, I promise you."

They sat in silence for a few minutes and then Jake leaned back in his chair again and grinned. "Can't believe you thought I was giving up so easily."

"Her hysterics were pretty convincing."

"Probably to make you feel bad." He chuckled. "Looks like it worked."

"Not funny." Lori slid off her shoes and settled back on the couch, legs tucked under her. "Would serve you right if she doesn't want to have anything more to do with you."

Jake shook his head. "Not possible. We're meant for each other."

"Don't take her for granted, Jake," Lori said, surprised by his unshakable confidence in her younger sister's feelings for him. "I'm sure she has plenty of guys in Cape Town who're in love with her."

Instead of looking worried, Jake smiled. "I know. She has but they don't matter."

"Wow. This is a side of you I've never seen before. I hope you're right, for your sake."

"It's time to take the next step." He leaned forward again. "In fact, one of the things I'm planning to do in Lusaka is to find a ring."

Lori's eyebrows shot up as she stared at him in astonishment. "That's a bit quick, don't you think?"

Despite her efforts to make things right, she felt the unbidden panic twist in the pit of her stomach.

He shook his head. "No. We both want this and we're not getting any younger, so what's the point of hanging around?" He was quiet for a moment. "She did make me really angry today—you both did, baiting each other like that in front of everyone. And disappointed, really disappointed. But it's not enough to make me walk away. You should know me better than that, Lor. I don't give up so easily."

"I should've known," Lori said in barely more than a whisper. "But does that mean you're giving up on me?" The lump in her throat made it difficult for her to talk.

"Never," he said quietly but fiercely. "And I won't have to," he added more gently. "I know you, Lor. This isn't who you are and it's not who Carla is, either, despite what you think. More than that, you've already lost your brother. I can't believe you're okay with losing one of your sisters as well . . . or me."

"I'm not," she whispered. "I'm not okay with that."

"Good, that's the first step."

"But there's so much . . ."

"Let it go, Lor—for all of our sakes, just let it all go. Stop keeping score. It's not important. Family is what's important. Family is God's gift and you Maguires are richer than most."

"We lost Tom."

"Even so, you're still richer."

"It takes two."

"Yes, it does. And you'll see, take the first step, and she'll be right there to meet you. I'm sure of that."

Lori took a deep breath. "I'm not." She slipped on her shoes and stood up abruptly. "I came to beg you not to break up with her so I don't have that on my head as well, and here you are lecturing *me* about making up with her. You're as bad as Dad."

He laughed as he stood and pulled her up into a bear hug. "Thanks for coming, friend. Proves what a big softy you are after all." He chuckled again. "Now, tell me what kind of ring she'll like."

"Diamond," Lori's voice was muffled against his chest.

"Hmm." Jake let her go and walked her to the door. "So maybe I'd better wait till I get down to South Africa to get it. And don't tell me, I know: I'll have to make sure it's been ethically mined." He turned back to face her before opening the door. "I remember she loved that ring of your Nana Lily's. What does it look like? You've got it, haven't you? Maybe I could have it copied or find something similar."

"Oh no, don't do that," Lori cried making Jake draw back in surprise. "She'd hate that, I'm sure. Anyway, you'll figure out what to do. It's late and I have to get back or else the folks will be worried. Have a good trip tomorrow. And please don't tell Carla I came here tonight, Jake. Promise."

"Okay, okay. I promise. Now go, I have to get up at four-thirty."

"Good night. Drive safe." She planted a quick kiss on his cheek.

"You too."

She trotted down the steps and opened the door of Paddy's jeep.

"Lor?"

She stopped and turned to look back at him, silhouetted against his house lights.

"Thanks for coming."

She smiled as she slammed the car door shut and turned the key in the ignition.

Chapter 16

Paddy accepted a second cup of coffee from Beth. The dining room was flooded with sunlight and the aroma of breakfast. The clatter of silver on china was thrown into noisy relief by the lack of conversation, unusual for the Maguires but each member of the family seemed lost in their own thoughts.

Paddy polished the lens of his reading glasses with his napkin, and opened the book that had been lying on the corner of the table next to him. He silently turned the pages, tilting his chin up and down as he perused the verses printed there, until he found what he was looking for. He cleared his throat with a loud *a-hem*, causing the four women seated around the table to glance up in unison, and then read aloud:

> *"Then Peter came to Jesus and asked, 'Lord, how many times shall I forgive my brother when he sins*

against me? Up to seven times?' Jesus answered, 'I tell you, not seven times, but seventy times seven.'"

"That's Matthew chapter eighteen," said Paddy, flipping pages, "and Mark eleven quotes Jesus saying:

'And when you stand praying, if you hold anything against anyone, forgive him, so that your Father in heaven may forgive you your sins.'"

Paddy removed his glasses, laid them on the table beside him and looked around the table. Carla, to his left, had her eyes fixed on her napkin that she was folding into progressively smaller triangles. Even though she was avoiding his gaze, he recognized the pain and shame evident in her slumped shoulders.

Lori, seated to his right on Beth's far side, was staring intently out the window opposite her. Her raised chin and straight back may have fooled most, but Paddy saw the twitch in her jaw and the give-away glimmer in her eye.

The wall clock ticked loudly in the silence. At last Paddy spoke, quietly but firmly.

"Our God and Father didn't throw people out into this world, every man unto himself. Instead, He gave each one of us a unit in which He intended us to live and grow and be: the family unit. *We* are a family. He gave us to each other to love and honor and respect each other, to help and support and be there for each other. We are God's *gift* to each other."

Silence. Beth reached out and gently squeezed his hand in hers. Encouraged by her gentle smile, he continued.

"I believe that each family unit has the potential to be what God intended it to be. Sadly, because mankind is so flawed, families aren't always the safe refuge they should be. Carla, in your job you've probably come to know better than any of us that there are far too many families that are pure hell, full of abuse and violence and fear. That's a sad and terrible fact of life, but thank God, that's not *our* family. Your mother and I thank Him every day for each other and for each and every one of you, because you're all so special and precious to us. Even though you two live far away and we don't get to see you as often as we'd like, we hold you very close. You are always in our thoughts and hearts and prayers. You know that."

Paddy paused and saw Lori dash a tear from her cheek and heard Carla sniff. He took a deep breath and ploughed on. "A long time ago, you two loved each other to bits. And then Tom left us . . ."

"He didn't leave us, Daddy; he was taken from us," Lori said.

"The Lord giveth, and the Lord taketh away," Paddy said gently, "and it's not for us to wonder why, no matter how devastating. We have to leave it to God, while we do our best to pick up the pieces and carry on. Mercifully, we weren't alone in that struggle because we had each other."

"Not all of us felt like that, Daddy," Carla said.

"How would you know? You were just a baby," Lori said.

"I was five years old, *not* a baby." Carla raised her eyes to glare at Lori. "And I remember it all, as if it were yesterday." In a whisper, she added, "I wish I didn't."

Paddy put his hand on Carla's arm, silencing her with a look. "Enough, you two. We're not arguing. I don't have any desire to go back over that awful time to try and dig up why each one of us reacted the way we did; that's not my point. I just want to say that from then on, Lori, you pulled away—from all of us but mostly from Carla. And *you*, Carla, were a hurt and confused little girl so you reacted to Lori's rejection in anger, and you've never forgiven her. I'm no psychologist or analyst, but your mother and I have agonized over this for years and we're pretty sure that's why you can barely say a civil word to each other, even though you're both intelligent grown women. But it stops here and now," he said sternly. "Do you hear me?" Paddy unwaveringly met his daughters' surprised stares.

"Yes, Dad," Lori and Carla muttered simultaneously.

"Okay," Paddy said, leaning back in his chair. "Now, your mother, Aunt Mae, and I are flying to Lusaka with Joe and the boys for a couple of days."

"What? When?" Carla exclaimed.

"We'll be leaving first thing in the morning," Paddy answered.

"What on earth for?" Lori asked Beth with a frown.

"Your Aunt Mae and I decided we'd go and do some shopping for my party."

While he knew that Beth was still in two minds regarding the trip, Paddy wanted his girls to know exactly where they stood. "We thought we'd leave the two of you to spend some time together. Hopefully, you'll both have the grace and maturity to talk and iron out your differences."

"Darlings, we're convinced that deep down, you'd both much rather be good friends and sisters—like the relationships you have with Becky. It's not so far-fetched," Beth said.

"But I'm warning you," Paddy continued his hard line, "you'd better make it happen, because I will *not* let your mother be embarrassed at her birthday party by the two of you. We will not have a repeat of Sunday's picnic."

"Oh, come on, Dad," Lori said.

"What if I want to come to Lusaka too?" Carla asked.

"Too bad." Paddy scraped his chair backwards and stood up. "No room in the plane."

"Is Becky going?"

"No, Lori, she's not; she says she's not up to the trip."

"Her due date is in a month, isn't it?" Aunt Mae spoke for the first time.

"Yes, about a couple of weeks after the party," Beth said as she stacked the used dishes onto a tray.

"Well, I think you're all mean," Carla said.

Paddy stooped to kiss the top of her head. "Call it tough love, sweetheart. You'll thank us for it one day."

"You've all lost it," Lori muttered as she loaded a second tray with the tea and coffee pots. "I didn't come all this way for you to disappear for days."

"Don't exaggerate darling," Beth said. "It's only for a couple of days. And anyway, we deserve a break."

Lori looked at her mother. "What do you mean by *that*?"

Beth met Lori's gaze and squared her shoulders. "It hasn't exactly been very pleasant around here with the two of you bitching at each other all the time."

"Beth!" Paddy was shocked at his normally mild-mannered wife's choice of words.

"Well, it's true. That's exactly what they've been doing ever since they got here. And I can't stand it anymore." She grabbed the milk jug and butter dish and marched out of the room.

Paddy took his hat off the peg by the door and turned to face his daughters who had been left standing open-mouthed with surprise at their mother's uncharacteristic outburst. Unsmiling, his voice was ominously low.

"Your behavior is hurting your mother and I won't have that. So get over yourselves already and fix this."

Jamming his hat on his head, he turned and left the room, Rex close at heel.

The morning passed quietly with Lori and Carla particularly subdued. Lori went for a swim, her body slicing through the cool water for length after length. Toweling herself down, she took a drink out of the bar fridge in the *lapa*, spread a sarong over one of the sunbeds and sat down, her legs outstretched. There she stayed for a long while, sipping her drink and staring out across the pool, lost in thought. Eventually, refreshed and feeling much calmer, she went back up to the house to shower and dress in time for lunch.

She found Beth, Mae, and Carla in the lounge where they'd spent much of the morning discussing the upcoming birthday party and making shopping lists for extras that they could now bring from town. Lori went through to the kitchen to see if she could help Jonas with lunch. Finding everything under control there and yet wanting to be busy, she went to lay the table in the dining room.

The tablecloth billowed out over the dark-wood table at a flick of Lori's arms. As she smoothed it, a little movement at the bottom of the garden caught her attention. The perimeter fence might have kept cattle and the occasional wild or rabid dog out but was no deterrent to the vervet monkeys that lived in the surrounding bush.

Lori stood motionless by the window, trying to see if she could catch another glimpse. Her patience was rewarded as after a few minutes, one of these beautiful and inquisitive little creatures sauntered out from behind the rockery. It sat still for a while on the grass, its dark face pointed in the direction of the house as it seemed to gauge whether or not it was safe to venture further. It was midday, the daily 'knock-off' time for all the farm workers who would go home for their midday meal, so all was quiet, no gardener or dogs to disturb.

The monkey began to walk and then lope across the lawn, slowly at first, and then faster as it approached the safety of the trees on the far side of the garden. It ran up the first large tree it came to, easily scaling its trunk and then leaping into its branches and the camouflage of its leafy covering.

Lori watched with delight as one by one the monkeys appeared from the same spot and either dashed or walked across the lawn toward the trees to join their friend. The large, heavier-set males led the way, followed by the medium-sized mamas with their babies either clinging to their stomachs or running nervously alongside them. The trees came alive as if blown by strong winds as the monkeys jumped from branch to branch, tree to tree, making their way around the garden boundary to the fruit trees beyond the pool and house.

"There's a *huge* troop of monkeys," called Lori excitedly as she headed through the lounge on her way to the bedroom wing. "Aunt Mae, come see."

The three women followed Lori into her bedroom from where they had a prime view of the frolicking monkeys. Just a short distance from the window a large flamboyant tree with a long, thick, low-hanging branch served as an easy launch pad to a guava tree. Its remaining fruit was still green but this didn't seem to bother the monkeys.

The bravest dropped down onto the ground next to the little tree, quickly plucking the green guavas and popping them into their mouths before scampering back up to a safer height. Perched on a higher branch, their long, skinny tails hanging straight down, they held the hard, green fruit in their tiny black hands, gnawing quickly and spitting out the bits they didn't want. The more timid among them simply crept as far out onto a branch as they could before pulling the leaves and fruit closer to them for easier pickings.

"Paddy will *not* be happy to see them," Beth said.

"But they're so cute," Aunt Mae said.

"They constantly pinch our fruit and a couple of weeks ago they utterly destroyed the green mealies in our veggie garden, leaving the broken stalks stripped bare."

"Oh dear," Aunt Mae said, pulling a face. "I bet that didn't go down too well."

"No, it didn't. He was livid," Beth said, "but it's hard to know what to do. I'm happy to see they're breeding and finding food, but it's a bit difficult when it's at our expense."

A few minutes later, the other women left the room but Lori quietly pulled the armchair out of the corner and closer to the window. It was the largest troop of vervets she'd ever seen. The trees were full of them, branches swaying and leaves rustling as they moved about, occasionally making *kek-kek-kek* sounds of warning in response to anything vaguely suspicious or threatening.

Enchanted, she watched them eat, jump and play, kiss, and then box each other's ears, scratch, and eat some more. Some hung upside down by their legs and tails, stretching their arms out for tasty morsels of seed pods or fallen fruit, while others sat back on their haunches for a leisurely scratch.

One mischievous little acrobat swung by his arm like a pendulum on a twisted bunch of twigs before suddenly dropping down to the lowest branch directly opposite Lori's bedroom window. Standing on his hind legs, he comically tipped his black, triangular little face with its fringe of white fur to one side, as if trying to figure out what he was seeing.

The rest of the troop began to move on. Slipping through or climbing over the far fence, they disappeared into the tall eucalyptus trees and bush beyond, their progress marked by the undulating branches. But the little monkey remained on the branch, bobbing up and down without breaking his fixed stare. Lori became anxious.

"Go on," she said. "Please don't be left behind."

The monkey looked around but made no move to go in search of his troop. Instead, he sat down on the branch and scratched his creamy-white stomach nonchalantly, tipping his little head to one side and then the other in a pantomime of curiosity. Lori was mesmerized and the two sat gazing at each other, as if in silent communion.

"You can't stay alone, sweetheart," she murmured. "You need your family . . ."

But the little vervet didn't heed her advice; he continued to sit and stare at her intently, his head extended forward as if to get as close as safely possible. As she stared back at him, a quiet yet startling thought dripped into her heart and rippled through her mind: "So do you, Lori, so do you."

Eventually, a few monkeys strolled and swung their way back, perhaps to collect their errant sibling. The spell was broken and he clambered up into the higher branches to join the others.

Lori watched the vervets for a bit longer before reluctantly tearing herself away to join the rest of her family for lunch. They'd almost finished without her but she didn't mind; it had been wonderful to watch the fascinating and playful little creatures, wild and free, as they should be.

She never mentioned her magic moment with the monkey.

Beth was setting the tray for tea later that afternoon when the front door burst open.

"Gran," Ben called, echoed by Riley. "Granny?"

"Here, in the kitchen," Beth said. "Hello my darlings. Have you come for tea?"

"No, 'fraid not," Joe said, appearing behind his boys. "Becky's waiting for us at home, so we won't stay. Just came by to finalize about tomorrow."

"Paddy's at the workshops or in his office, I think, if you want to speak to him."

Right on cue, Paddy strode across the quad, stopping to pull off his boots by the kitchen door. "Joe, how are you son? All set for tomorrow?"

"Ja, all good, thanks Dad. Just on my way back from the *boma*, so I thought I'd call in to see that we're coordinated and good for take-off at seven-thirty, latest."

"Yes, that sounds fine," Paddy said. "Hello boys. Who's sitting next to Grandpa in the plane tomorrow?"

"Me, me!" Riley yelled, jumping up and down in front of his grandfather.

"Ah, that's good to know. And are you going to help your Dad read the instruments up front, Ben?"

"Dad said he'd let me hold the yoke tomorrow." Ben beamed.

"When it's on auto-pilot," Joe said quickly. "Did you notice the clouds building up, Paddy?"

"Yes, I did. Looks like a December sky out there. Strange."

"We've had storms in April before. Remember the freak storm we had a couple of years ago in April? Thunder, lightning, the works."

"I hope that's not going to happen. Will it be alright to fly?" Beth felt a twinge of nervousness as she poured boiling water into the large tea-pot.

"We'll see what happens tonight. It may just circle us and blow away," Joe said. "It's happened before. But the earlier we take off the smoother flight we should have."

"We'll be there by seven," Paddy said.

"Come on boys, let's go. Mum's waiting."

"How is Becky, dear?" Beth asked.

"She's tired so she's been taking it easy today," Joe said. "Actually, I wanted to ask Lori and Carla if they could perhaps go over and spend the night with her tomorrow."

"Yes, of course," Lori said as she came into the kitchen. "I was going to call her and suggest that anyway."

"The problem with Becky is she'll tell you there's no need for you to bother, but I'm asking you to go anyway, if you don't mind. Even if she says you don't have to."

"Sure, don't worry about it. We'll be there." She turned to her father. "You are leaving us a car, aren't you, Dad?"

"You'll have Mum's car," Paddy said, "and there's the farm truck as well. You know where the keys are."

"If you could just make sure they've got full tanks, that would be great."

"I'll check straight after tea," Paddy said.

Joe was chivvying his boys out the front door.

"See you tomorrow, boys," Beth said. "Give our love to your Mum."

"Joe."

Carla had been reading in the *lapa* after a swim and had heard the jeep. Her heart leaped and then thumped hard as she sat waiting, expecting Jake to appear on the verandah and come striding down the lawn toward her. But he didn't so after a few minutes she wrapped a towel around her and walked quickly up and around the side of the house.

"Joe," she called again.

Joe stopped and turned, told the boys to get in the car and waited for Carla.

"Have you seen Jake today?" she asked, hurrying towards him.

He shook his head.

"Do you know where he is? Is he at home?"

"No, he's not. He's gone to town for a couple of days."

"What, to Lusaka? I didn't know. Will you see him there?"

"Bit of a spontaneous trip, I think," Joe said. "Maybe we'll meet up but I'm not sure. We'll all be pretty busy."

"Okay." Carla looked away and then back at him. "Did you speak to him? Is he . . . is he really mad?"

With a sigh, Joe turned and started to walk to his vehicle. "I'm not getting into this, Carla. I'm sorry, I have to get home to Becky, but . . ." He turned back to face her. "I'll tell you this for nothing: if you want to be with Jake, you have to clear things up with Lori."

Carla's jaw tightened. "It shouldn't matter so much."

Joe shook his head and looked at her with an expression of pity that annoyed Carla even more.

"You know Jake," he said. "He hates being around strife and anger and bickering more than anything. So, he's certainly not going to accept it as his lot in life just because you and Lori insist on behaving like a couple of tantrumming brats."

Carla bit her lip; his words stung. She was very fond of her brother-in-law who'd known her most of her life; his opinion mattered and he didn't seem to have a very high one of her right now.

Joe shook his head again and climbed up into the jeep where his boys were tussling in the back seat. "It's your choice, Carla," he called out the open window as his wheels crunched the gravel toward the gate. "What's it going to be?"

Carla remained motionless where he'd left her, clutching the bunched corners of the towel to her chest. She realized with a sickening ache in the pit of her stomach that it was more or less in this very spot that Jake had kissed her less than forty-eight hours ago. She had felt at that moment as though her heart would burst with happiness, as she'd finally admitted to herself—and him—how crazy in love with him she was. They had agreed to show their love off to the world, to commit. Now, those enchanted moments seemed like a lifetime ago.

She slowly returned to her chair by the pool. *It's your choice, Carla.* Joe's voice echoed in her head. She knew he was right. It was easier to blame Lori for everything, to let the ache turn into anger. She'd done it for most of her life. Could she really forgive her? Was she capable of making that choice? Not in her own power, she was sure.

Then, her thoughts turned a corner, one that she'd never considered or perhaps never allowed herself to acknowledge before. Did Lori have things to forgive *her* for? She'd been so focused on always being the victim she'd never considered there may be two victims here, two aggressors.

"Oh, dear God, help me," Carla whispered and then quickly pasted on a smile to meet her mother and Aunt Mae who were making their way down to the *lapa*, Paddy and Lori close behind with the tea-trays.

Lori voluntarily cut and handed Carla a piece of cake, and Carla murmured her thanks without a hint of sarcasm. Although the mood was a far cry from festive it was at least civil, and Carla suddenly felt a glimmer of hope.

They'd hardly finished tea when the garden trees began to sway and swish, this time not because of the antics of cavorting monkeys but rather because they were harassed by a strong wind that had suddenly blown in, pushing heavy grey clouds in front of it.

Much later, there were no moon or stars to be seen in the African night sky, only the occasional flash of lightning piercing the heavy blackness, intermittently followed by ominous rumblings of thunder. Carla shivered, pulling her robe closer and moved away from the verandah doors where she'd been standing.

But there was no rain. Not that night.

Part Three

"You may be as different as the sun and the moon, but the same blood flows through both your hearts. You need her, as she needs you."

George. R.R. Robert

Chapter 17

Lori padded along the quad-side passageway toward Beth's kitchen, the terracotta tiles cold under her bare feet. Its heavy wooden door was open and latched to the outside passage wall, allowing the smell of warm toast and fresh coffee to waft across the quad and into the bedrooms.

She found Paddy and Aunt Mae seated at the kitchen island munching marmalade-lathered toast. Carla sat at the far end, sipping coffee out of an enormous mug. Like Lori, she was dressed in her robe, her hair still messy from sleep.

"Morning darling!" Beth said cheerily as she carried more toast over to the breakfasters. "Did we wake you?"

"It's alright." Lori headed for the coffee pot. "What time are you leaving?"

"Six thirty." Paddy glanced at the wall clock. "Twenty minutes. Come on girls," he chivvied Beth and Mae. "Nearly time to leave."

"Don't hassle me, Paddy," Beth said. "You can go and put the bags in the car if you want. I need to talk to the girls first." She turned to Lori and Carla. "Now, I've told Jonas to take a couple of days off, until we're back. He's not going anywhere, so he'll be around if you need him but I thought he could do with the break before the party. And besides, he'll enjoy the extra time with his new grandson."

"Good idea." Lori set her coffee mug down and pulled back a chair to sit down.

"That's fine," Carla agreed.

"You'll manage without him, won't you?" Beth asked. "Besides, I thought you may well go over to Becky's for the whole time, not just tonight."

"But if you do that," Paddy said, "be sure to tell Jonas so he knows to come feed the dogs and make sure they're alright. He'll also let Fred know and check the gates are locked at night."

"Okay, got it." Lori blew the steam off her coffee.

Paddy gave a buttered crust to each of the dogs waiting expectantly at his feet.

"Spoiler," Carla said.

"They deserve it." Paddy let Rex lick the butter off his fingers.

"Beth, Mae, I'll meet you at the car in . . ." Paddy paused at the door to check his watch, "five minutes."

"Bye Daddy," Carla called after him, whereupon Paddy reappeared to embrace both his daughters.

"Keep an eye on Becky," he told Carla, and to Lori, "Use the time well." Then he and Rex were out the door and walking across the quad towards his office.

"Come on Mae, we really do have to get moving, otherwise he'll drive like a crazy man to reach Joe's airstrip on time."

"Leave the breakfast things and go, Mum," Carla said. "We'll clear up."

"Make yourselves a proper breakfast, please girls. You haven't eaten anything."

"It's too early," Lori said. "Off you go mother hen. We promise to eat copious amounts while you're gone." She was amused by her mother's fussing, wondering if she'd also treat Jonathan and Noya like ten-year-old's when they were in their forties.

Ten minutes later, bags and passengers loaded into the car and final goodbyes said, they were off, through the gate and up the long driveway, trailed by a cloud of red dust. Lori, Carla, and the dogs stood on the front porch, watching them go until they couldn't see them anymore.

Carla turned back into the house but Lori remained where she was and studied the skies; they seemed clearer now although there was still a brisk breeze. Perhaps it had blown the threat of rain away. She returned to the kitchen where Carla was pouring herself another mug of coffee.

"I'm taking this back to bed," she said. "I didn't sleep so well last night."

"Okay," Lori said "Have a lie-in. I'll probably go for a run. I'll take Rex with me."

Carla nodded. Lori was surprised how easy it was to chat rather than bicker, and wondered if Carla felt the same. Maybe this *is* actually possible, she thought as she replaced the lids on the marmalade pot and butter dish and carried them over to the fridge.

Lori ran along familiar paths through the bush with Rex at her heels, each step kicking childhood memories up out of the dust. About an hour later, as they trotted a cooling jog down the red-brown road home, Lori noticed clouds building up again, rolling and dark grey in patches. The winds that were agitating the trees brought with them a whiff of rain.

Damp with sweat, she quickly changed and went down to the pool. Dropping her towel on a sunbed, she stood at the edge of the pool and scanned the sky for any signs of lightning before diving in. After a few lengths, she pulled herself out of the water, looking up and around at the fickle skies. She felt uneasy. The wind was rattling leaves and twigs across the lawns and flower beds in a disquieting manner. Wrapping the towel around her as she walked, Lori headed up to the house to shower.

A little while later, Lori sat on the stool in front of her dressing table, set her mobile phone down and tapped in Becky's number. She activated the speaker and listened to the ring-tone while towel-drying her hair, but the seconds ticked by and Becky didn't answer. She felt the twisting uneasiness again in the pit of her stomach.

"Hello?"

"Becky," Lori exclaimed with relief. "I was beginning to get worried."

"Sorry, I was doing the laundry and my phone was in the lounge. Almost didn't hear it."

"You're meant to be resting," Lori said.

"Yes, I've had an early lunch and I'm going to have a lie-down now," Becky said. "I've been having lots of Braxton-Hicks contractions yesterday and today, so I'm taking it easy."

"Really? Are you sure they're Braxton-Hicks and not the real thing?"

Becky laughed. "Sometimes it's difficult to tell, but I've got another month to go, and it was like this before I had Riley as well."

Lori wasn't convinced. "I'm coming over."

"Well, I was expecting you at some stage," Becky said. "Joe said you'd both come for the night, which'd be wonderful . . . not to mention miraculous." She laughed.

Lori ignored her insinuation. "Of course we'll stay the night."

"Are you getting on okay together over there, or are you killing each other?"

"We're fine. We even said a few civil words to each other this morning."

"You're kidding," Becky said.

"Yeah, who'd have believed?" Lori chuckled. "Anyway, I'll find Carla and come over just now, okay?"

"Don't feel you have to rush. I'm really okay."

"Go lie down now and we'll see you in a bit."

"Will do. Thanks, Lor."

"Bye, darling."

Lori finished dressing and went in search of Carla. There was no answer to her calls so she walked down to the bedroom door at the very end of the passage.

"Carla?" She knocked on the door before opening it.

Carla was sitting on the edge of her bed tying the laces of one of her running shoes.

"Ah, here you are. I've just spoken to Becky and I'm worried about her."

"Why?" Carla looked up with a frown.

"Well, she sounded a bit breathless, for starters. And she said she's having lots of Braxton-Hicks contractions."

"I remember she had the same before Riley's birth." Carla pulled on her other shoe. "Mum kept having hysterics that she wouldn't get to Lusaka on time because there wasn't any really decent clinic around here then. But in the end, she made it to the full forty weeks."

"Hmm, that's what she said. But still, I feel a bit anxious and it looks like it's going to pour with rain any minute."

Perching on the arm of the corner chair, Lori looked around her sister's bedroom, not sure when she'd last been in here. It was a pleasant room, the same size as hers, more or less, with the same large window. The décor was blue and white and cream, with a distinctly seaside motif that managed to be sophisticated at the same time. Suddenly, the watery feel to the room struck Lori as ironic, and she shivered.

"I know we said we'd go over there this afternoon but I think we should go over now," Lori said, walking back to the door.

"But I'm on my way out for a run," Carla said. "I slept all morning, which is ridiculous; can't remember when I last did that. I need to go out and clear my head a bit."

"I already took Rex with me for an hour's run, so he probably won't want to go again."

"I'll go without him."

"You can go for a run at Becky's."

"No," Carla said firmly. "I don't know their farm as well, so don't like the thought of running there on my own." She stood and faced Lori. Old Toffee, who'd been slumbering on her bedside mat, struggled up and came to stand beside them, wagging her tail. "Why don't you go ahead? I'll go for my run and come later, after I've fed the dogs."

Lori gave up. "Okay, I will, but please don't go for a swim," she said. "It looks like a bad storm brewing out there, so it won't be safe."

Carla's eyebrows arched as if with surprise to hear concern in Lori's voice. "Alright, I won't."

"Keep your phone on you," Lori said, "and don't forget to call Jonas before you leave to tell him we've gone. Hopefully, he'll come check on the dogs. Which car do you prefer?"

"You take Mum's car," Carla said, pulling her hair up into a pony-tail as she left her room. "I'll bring the truck. See you later," she called without looking back as she passed Paddy's locked office on her way to the back door.

Lori walked into the middle of the quad and looked up at the threatening skies. She realized that this was the longest conversation she'd had with Carla for many, many years.

Chapter 18

The first giant drop of rain hit the windscreen with a crack that made Lori jump just as she was edging down the slope toward the wooden bridge on her way to Becky's. Leaning forward, she peered up at the sky for a second and frowned at the now ominously black clouds.

Another drop of rain, and another, and another. The crack-crack-crack quickly became a steady drum beat, and she had to slow to a crawl as she strained to see the bridge beyond the nose of the car even though the windscreen wipers were flicking back and forth as fast as they could. She gripped the wheel, white-knuckled, as she drove on down.

She was alarmed to see the great tree's tortured convulsions on the river's edge as the wind bent it angrily this way and that with great creaks and groans. The river, whipped into waves, licked at its roots as it rushed and tossed beneath the bridge.

Lori held her breath as the car clattered over the wooden planks, then breathed a sigh of relief once she was safely on the other side and accelerating up the hill towards the house. Bringing the car to a stop outside the back door, she dashed for cover.

"Becky," she called, laughing as she stood dripping in the kitchen, toeing off her sneakers. "I'm here. Crazy weather out there. You should see the old tree."

Silence.

"Becks?" Lori padded barefoot into the lounge, expecting to see her sister sleeping on the couch, but she wasn't.

"Becky?" She walked quickly down the passageway toward the master bedroom, leaving wet footprints on the polished tiles.

The door was open so Lori walked straight in. The cover looked slightly rumpled but the bed was empty. Lori felt the coil of uneasiness that had been sitting in the pit of her stomach for most of the day writhe up in unleashed panic. The en-suite bathroom was also empty, so she ran from room to room through the house, calling her sister again and again, but Becky was nowhere to be seen.

Back in the lounge, she noticed the sliding doors were open, the curtains on either side billowing in the wind. How hadn't she noticed that before? She ran out onto the verandah and called again.

"Becky, where are you?" But the wind whipped her voice away.

It was hard to hear anything over the noise of the rain drumming on the roof of the house and splattering onto the edges of the verandah floor. But was that a bark? She started calling the dogs' names while running down the stone steps and out into the garden. The barking grew louder until Joe's Rottweiler came bounding up to her from behind the hedge of the vegetable garden.

"Good boy," Lori yelled above the storm. "Where's Becky? Where's Becky?" The dog jumped up at her and barked again, then whirled and raced back in the direction from where he'd come. Lori ran after him.

She found Becky lying next to the vegetable garden hedge with her faithful German shepherd dog close beside her, licking her face as she whined and nudged her.

"Becky!" Lori cried as she fell to her knees next to her sister. To her enormous relief, Becky opened her eyes.

"Lor?"

Lori could see rather than hear her mouth her name. "What on earth are you doing out here?"

"Pain . . ." Becky tried to blink the rain out of her eyes as she looked up at Lori.

"Don't speak, darling. Let's just get you out of the rain. Can you get up? You *have* to get up, Becky." She struggled to keep the panic out of her voice.

Pumped with adrenalin, Lori heaved Becky up until she was on her feet. She was wobbly, but with Lori's support and sheer determination, they managed to make it back inside the house and down the corridor to the bedroom, the dripping, whining dogs close on their heels all the way.

Lori eased Becky onto her bed and looked down at her, soaking wet and pale-faced against the pillows. Lori tried to remain calm and prioritize.

"Tell me quickly, Becky, what happened?" she asked as she covered her with a quilt.

"Labor . . . pains." Becky gasped and her eyes flew open as she moaned and then stifled a scream.

Lori sat down next to her and took hold of her hand. "Squeeze me." With her free hand, she pulled her phone out of her pocket and called Carla.

The ring tone seemed to go on and on. "Come on, Carla," she whispered. "Now is *not* the time to ignore me."

It cut off into the no-answer message. She called again, and then again. Finally, Carla answered.

"Hello?"

"Carla, for goodness' sake." She couldn't keep the irritation out of her voice.

"What? I just got home from my run. I didn't hear it ring."

"Becky's gone into labor. I found her in the garden, in the rain. There's no time to explain. Just get over here now, please."

"What? It's not raining here," Carla said. "Did you say she's gone into labor? Is she having contractions?"

"Yes."

"How far apart?"

"I don't know, Carla. I haven't been with her long enough to measure, but I'll start counting. Please, just get in the car now and come here. Don't shower or anything, there's no time." Dropping the phone on the bed, she turned back to Becky. "You poor thing," she said, stroking her damp face. "How long were you out there?"

Becky just groaned and shut her eyes.

A few minutes later, Lori's phone rang. It was Carla. "I'm on my way. I'm bringing Mom's medical bag, just in case. How is she?"

"I noted the time at the end of the last contraction," Lori said, tapping the phone into speaker mode so she could talk while she changed Becky out of her wet clothes and toweled her hair dry. "So I'll know how far apart when the next one starts."

"Good," Carla said. "Please call Jonas and tell him I've left and he needs to take care of the dogs."

"Okay. Oh, ow, here we go," Lori said as Becky gripped her hand and cried out.

"It's about seven minutes since the last one," Lori said eventually when Becky had dropped back against the pillow, breathing heavily.

"That's close," Carla said. "Keep her calm and help her to breathe through the contractions. Maybe get her to pant in between. That'll hopefully slow them down. I'll be there as quickly as I can. And leave Jonas, I'll call him. You just be with Becky."

"Drive carefully, Carla. You'll be coming into the rain, if you haven't already. Don't go and have an accident, please."

"The skies are crazy black, and I see it coming this way, an absolute sheet. Talk about a fluke storm."

"Careful over the bridge," Lori said. "I'm going to try call the doctor now. See you in a bit."

Lori found the doctor's number in Becky's phone and listened impatiently to the continuing ring tone. Frustrated, she dialed the district hospital instead.

"Hello?" someone answered at last.

"Hello. Can I speak to Dr. Solomon please? It's an emergency."

"Dr. Solomon is not here," the cheery voice said.

"Where is he?"

"He is in Lusaka. He will be back next week."

"Well, is there *another* doctor? I have an emergency here."

"And what is your emergency?"

"My sister, Becky, has started her labor. Becky Blackwell."

"Mrs. Blackwell? But she is only meant to be having her baby in a month's time."

"I know, we're all very surprised. But I really need a doctor, now."

"I think you must bring Mrs. Blackwell here. I will call the midwife and tell her to come to the hospital so she will be waiting for you."

"My other sister is on her way here," Lori said. "She's also a midwife. We'll bring her in together, just make sure you're ready for us. Thank you." She tossed the phone aside and clenched her teeth as Becky's nails dug into her hand with the force of another contraction.

Turning her full attention to Becky, she encouraged her to breathe through the pain, silently marveling that she remembered the breathing techniques from her own long-ago births. Fixing a smile on her face and shooting arrow prayers for Carla's quick arrival and Becky and the baby's safety, she did her best to act with a calm she didn't feel.

Two contractions later, Lori heard the truck, the noise of its engine faint against the backdrop of the storm.

"Carla's nearly here, sweetheart." She smiled at Becky, stroking the strands of hair from her pale, strained-looking face, before standing up. "I'll be back in a minute."

Becky nodded and closed her eyes.

Lori ran into the lounge just as Carla burst into the room from the kitchen door, black bag in hand.

"Is the doctor on his way?" Carla asked, shedding her jacket.

"No, he's away in Lusaka, if you can believe it," Lori said as she went to close the verandah doors against the windy gusts of leaves and rain. She hadn't stopped to close them before, when she'd struggled through them with Becky. "We'll have to take her there. So, I think you should check her quickly, and if we're good to—"

A sudden, ear-splitting bang made them both shriek as a streak of lightning flashed down from the heavy, dark clouds. Its vein-like forks hit the old tree by the bridge in a blue-white explosion, splitting it in two. The sisters watched in open-mouthed astonishment as the mangled tree creaked like a giant wooden door being pushed open for the first time in a hundred years, and then crashed over the far end of the bridge.

"Daddy was right," Lori whispered eventually.

"Oh, my goodness. We . . . we can't take Becky . . ." Carla stammered.

Lori turned to stare at her as the full effect of the lightning strike on their immediate situation sunk in.

"What'll we do?" She felt the sickening fear rise up inside her again.

Carla paused for a second and then squared her shoulders. "We'll work together and we'll deliver this baby," she said.

"*What?*" Lori exclaimed in a loud whisper. She didn't want Becky to hear although it was highly unlikely that she could hear anything over the noise of the storm. "I can't do that, Carla. I've never delivered a baby."

"I'm a midwife," Carla whispered back, "and I've delivered many babies, all of them safely."

"But that was in a *hospital*. With doctors. What if there are complications?"

"Lori, get a grip. The only choice we have is to work together and do this. And we *can* do this, *if* we work together." Carla grasped Lori's arms and looked into her eyes. "We have to put everything else aside and work together—for Becky and the baby. Can we do that?"

Lori stared back at her for a few seconds and then shook herself slightly. "Yes, yes of course we can."

"Good. But you have to listen to me. And if I tell you to do something, I'm not being bossy, I'm being a midwife. So please don't fight with me. Okay?"

Tears pricked Lori's eyes. She realized the thing she most wanted to do was hug Carla, but she restrained herself. Becky was waiting.

"Yes, boss," she said and smiled.

"Good." Carla matched Lori's smile. "So, let's go do this."

They ran down the corridor, picking up speed as they heard Becky cry out in pain.

"Where have you been?" a red-faced Becky growled at them. "I want to go to the hospital now. And don't leave me to have another contraction alone."

Lori and Carla exchanged a look before Lori gently explained to Becky about the tree.

"So, you see Becks, we can't take you to the hospital and the doctor can't get here, but we're good," she finished with feigned brightness.

"How . . . exactly . . . are we good?" Becky panted and then started to cry as she sank back against the pillows.

"Well, my darling, for starters our sister happens to be an excellent midwife." Lori sat beside her on the bed and stroked her face and hair. "She's going to take great care of you and she's going to deliver your baby. Everything's going to be fine, Becky, I promise. You just need to relax and rest when you can and listen to Carla. We're going to do everything she tells us to and we're going to get through this together. And you know what? I'm sure it's going to be the most special birth ever."

Lori's own confidence grew as she spoke softly and soothingly to Becky who visibly calmed down.

"Oh, dear God," Becky breathed, "help them deliver my baby safely, please."

Lori murmured a quiet "amen" as she bent to kiss her forehead.

Carla opened her mother's medical bag on the couch under the window. Lori saw her clench then shake out her hands and saw her lips move in whispered prayer. Carla stood for a few seconds longer, gazing out the picture window at the gusts of rain still sweeping across the garden and then held her hands out in front of her, palms down. They were steady as rock as she turned to face her sisters with a look of quiet confidence.

"Lori, please bring a few clean towels and a couple of extra sheets while I wash my hands."

Lori hurried to the linen cupboard while Carla continued to direct matters from the bathroom. "Becks, do you have one of those plastic under-sheets from when the boys were little? Tell Lori where she can find one, please, and then we'll just reorganize your bed a bit," she said, drying her hands on a clean towel as she re-entered the room.

Removing the blood pressure kit from her mother's bag, she wrapped the band around Becky's upper arm. "Have your waters broken already?"

Her matter-of-fact and professional manner had the desired calming effect on Becky who nodded and then reached up and touched Carla's cheek.

"I'm so glad you're here," she whispered.

Carla smiled down at her as she plugged the stethoscope into her ears and placed its cool disc on Becky's bared bulge. "No place on earth I'd rather be right now, Becks."

Lori laid the pile of towels and sheets on the couch under the window so they'd be within easy reach, and then shook out the plastic under-sheet she'd found.

"I'll remake Joe's side of the bed with this and some clean sheets, and then we can move Becky over. Okay?"

"Yes, absolutely, thanks," Carla said, looping the stethoscope around her neck. "Baby's heart is sounding strong, Becks. You're doing so well."

Once Becky was settled on the other side of the bed, Carla started a more thorough examination.

"I'm going to go and call Joe and the folks," Lori said, leaving the room.

"Can you bring water for us all to drink, please?" Carla asked. "With straws and ice for Becky."

Lori paused at the door and looked back at the scene. Just moments before, it had been fraught with tension and a sense of panic; now, everything was under control, and a sense of sweet anticipation was beginning to pervade the room. Becky's color looked better and she'd stopped crying. It had even stopped raining, Lori realized, as she heard the drip-drip-drip of the run-off from the trees and roof gutters outside.

"Lor?" Carla had turned to see her still standing at the door. "Please hurry back, because we're going to need your help here in a little while."

"Can't do this without you, babe," Becky muttered with a weak smile.

Lori turned away silently, a large lump jamming her throat against any words she might have spoken. Carla hadn't called her Lor since she'd been a tiny girl. She suddenly felt that despite the drama of the afternoon something had come right in the world; a disconnection had clicked back into place, and she felt filled with a quiet peace and deep joy that was totally new to her.

She made her way to the kitchen, bringing up Joe's number on her mobile phone as she went.

"Joe? Hi, Lori here." She pulled a jug of cold water out of the fridge and grabbed glasses out of a cupboard. Now, where could she find straws?

"Lots to tell you, hon, but quick and to the point. Don't panic but Becky's gone into labor . . . Here at your house. She's okay, doing well . . . No, Dr. Solomon is in Lusaka . . . No, we can't take her to the hospital . . . Because there's been a terrible storm and the tree by the bridge was hit by lightning . . . Yes, it fell onto the bridge. I don't know about broken but it's definitely totally blocked . . . Daddy was right. You should know that by now; sooner or later, he's always right . . . Yes, obviously it's too late for you to fly back now; Becky wouldn't hear of it. You'll be back in the morning? Okay. I'll call you as soon as there's news, I promise. Joe, Joe, don't panic. There's nothing to worry about . . . Well, because Carla's here, and she's got everything under control. Yes, I promise, we'll take good care of her."

As she pushed through the swing door from kitchen to lounge, loaded tray of glasses, ice and water in hand, Lori was struck by the sudden quiet and paused to look outside. The wind had died down, and a soft drip-dripping and the distant rush of the river were the only sounds she could hear.

The golden glow of an undefeated setting sun transformed the wet lawn into a carpet of a million, sparkling diamonds. Lori laid the tray down on the coffee table, slid the glass doors open and went out onto the verandah. She wasn't disappointed.

"Oh, wow."

She stood transfixed, drinking in the sight of the double rainbow crowning the bush on the far side of the river, vivid against a dramatic backdrop of dark-grey skies. She breathed a prayer of thanks and hoped she would always remember the view of this beautiful sign of an eternal promise.

The storm was over.

Chapter 19

Baby Lucy Blackwell was born at half past eight that Tuesday evening, the day of the great April storm. With a shock of black hair, pale white skin, rosebud mouth, and eyes tightly shut, she was a two-and-a-half kilo package of perfection.

Carla expertly coaxed Lucy into the world and once she'd taken her first breath, gently placed her tiny body in her mother's waiting arms. The stress of the day and all feelings of pain and exhaustion momentarily disappeared as Becky smiled down at the wonder lying against her breast. She stroked her cheek with one shaky finger and Lucy's newborn grey-blue eyes opened to stare back at her, unblinking.

"Welcome to our world, little Lucy," Becky whispered as Lori snapped photos and video clips with her phone and sent them to Joe in-between calls to him and the rest of the family in Lusaka. Becky blew kisses along with promises to speak later, not wanting anything to interrupt these first few moments with her long-awaited daughter.

A short while later, Carla clamped the umbilical cord. Removing her surgical gloves, she went into the bathroom to wash her hands.

"Shall I go make tea while you two finish up here?" Lori asked.

"I'd love some, but not yet," Becky said. "I want you both to come and sit here with Lucy and me for a couple of minutes. She wants to meet her two stellar aunties, don't you baby girl?" Becky cooed.

Lucy snuffled around Becky's breast, chick-like mouth open, until she found what she was looking for—with a little help from Becky—and latched on.

Lori and Carla obediently joined them on the bed, one on either side of Becky.

"You did incredibly well, Becky. I'm so proud of you," Lori said.

"I couldn't have done it without the two of you," Becky said, wincing slightly at her baby's suckling.

"We couldn't have done it without *Carla*," Lori said.

"I . . . I just don't know what I would have done if you hadn't been here. It's a terrifying thought." Becky's eyes brimmed with emotion.

"Well, we were here, darling," Lori said matter-of-factly, "so no need to think about it."

"You were right, Lori. It was the most amazing birth experience. Thank you so much. I can't tell you how grateful I am," Beth said with a sob, tears running unchecked down her cheeks.

"Don't be silly," Carla whispered. "I should be thanking *you*." She touched Lucy's clenched fist and her face lit up when the tiny fingers opened, one by one, like the petals of a little flower, and re-clenched around her finger. "It always amazes me, the miracle of birth, but this was so incredibly *extra*-special, to be here with both of you and deliver my own beautiful baby niece." She leant forward and kissed the little hand.

"I couldn't have asked for a better midwife," Becky said. "And you, Lori, are the best birthing partner any woman could wish for, although you'd better not tell Joe I said that."

"Carla," Lori said, "you should never stop doing this work. You are an *awesome* midwife."

Carla nodded. "I stopped a couple of years ago because I moved into social work; I thought that was my calling. And then I come here and *bam*, two births in a week. Now I remember how much I loved it. But *this* birthing experience is going to take some beating."

"Your own experience, Carla, when you have your own baby—that's what'll beat it," Becky said. "I hope you and Jake won't wait too long before starting a family."

Carla kissed Lucy's hand again before gently loosening her finger from its clasp and standing up.

"That's not going to happen," she said quietly. "Haven't you heard? It's over." Her voice reverted to professional mode. "Lori, I'd love that cup of tea now, if it's still on offer. We've got some things to do here to finish up properly. And when Lucy has stopped guzzling, I need to check her again quickly, and then we can get you both bathed and off to sleep."

"What are you talking about? What happened?" Becky looked wide-eyed from Lori to Carla.

Lori shrugged.

"Please Becks, don't spoil tonight for me," Carla pleaded. "I really don't want to talk about it."

"Okay," Becky said with a sigh of resignation. "But only for tonight." She leant back against the pillows, suddenly realizing how utterly exhausted she was.

Lori padded back into Becky's bedroom with two fleece rugs she'd found in the linen cupboard. Tossing one to Carla, she sat at the opposite end of the couch, stretching her legs out alongside Carla's and flicking the rug over them. She settled back against the cushions and looked at her sister. They'd left the curtains open so the moon, burning bright in the now cloudless sky, bathed the room in an ethereal light.

The last details of the birth taken care of, Carla had washed and dressed Becky and Lucy, while Lori had remade the bed with fresh sheets. Now, mother and baby were nestled together, fast asleep. The crib, standing empty in the corner of the room, would be prepared and placed next to Becky's side of the bed tomorrow—plenty of time for that. Tonight, they would stay as close to each other as possible.

Lori and Carla listened to Becky's even breathing and smiled at the occasional snuffling noises made by their new baby niece.

"She's so gorgeous," Lori whispered at last. "Joe's going to go crazy for her."

"She's absolutely going to wrap him around her tiny finger," Carla said.

"Like you and Daddy," Lori said, but without any trace of malice.

Carla smiled and nodded, gazing out the window at the garden beyond. Turning back to face Lori she said, "We worked well together tonight. You were a great help."

It was Lori's turn to smile. "Yeah, we made a good team, I reckon. Who'd have thought?"

Carla nodded again silently and looked down at her clasped hands.

"We've wasted an awful lot of years, Carla," Lori whispered. It was time to get this out in the open, to finish the feud.

Carla looked up to meet her sister's gaze. Lori noticed the dark smudges under Carla's eyes and cleared her throat softly. This wasn't easy but it had to be done. "I'm sorry," she said. "It wasn't your fault Tom died—you must never think that. I was just desperate to find someone to blame."

"Why? Why me?" Carla's voice broke and she dashed a tear from her face.

"Because he loved you so much. And you cried so much after the . . . the accident. You kept asking me where he was and I couldn't bear it. In a twisted teenage rage, instead of loving you and trying to help you understand, I pushed you away." Lori didn't wipe away the tears that were beginning to trickle down her own cheeks; she felt a cleansing as they flowed. "I've thought about it, the pain I must have caused you, the *extra* pain. You lost us both, and I'm so sorry. I was just so *angry*."

"Who with?" Carla whispered.

Lori thought for a little while before answering. "With Mum and Dad, I guess. With God, *definitely* for many, many years. And you. I was angry with you too."

"I still don't understand why," Carla said with a small sob. She sounded like a little girl, desperate and rejected but finally able to speak her mind.

Suddenly, it was all very clear to Lori. "Because you were the last one to see him. Because he was so crazy about you, he adored you. Because you have his eyes."

"So do you, silly," Carla said with a tearful sniff.

"Whenever I looked at you, I was reminded of him and . . . it was just too painful." Lori's chest heaved and shuddered as the walls she'd thrown up so many years ago came crashing down, and she tried to stifle her sobs so as not to wake up Becky. "He was a part of me—the breath in my lungs, the thoughts in my head. He was half my heart, my life . . . and then he was gone. Without even saying goodbye," she sobbed. "*Gone*. The world stopped for me and it was easier to hate everybody or at least try to make them hurt like I was hurting. Oh God, how awful I was. I must have made it so much harder for Mum and Dad." She'd never opened up to anyone to this extent before, not even Yoni, and although it felt unbearably painful, it was unexpectedly cathartic.

Carla nodded silently, her own tears continuing to drip.

"And you must have been so *devastated*, poor baby. I'm sorry, Carla, I'm so sorry."

Lori leaned towards Carla who sat cross-legged, her face now buried in her hands. Knees to knees, Lori reached out and put her arms around Carla's shoulders and drew her close.

"When I realized what I'd done to you," Lori said, "when I started struggling out of my fog and trying to rebuild my life—thanks to Yoni and no doubt a lot of prayer—it was too late. You hated me. Really hated me. And I didn't blame you. I deserved it. So, I kept playing the game: rejection for rejection."

Lori felt her shoulder grow damp from Carla's tears. "Oh, sweetheart, I'm so sorry," she whispered into Carla's hair, thinking she'd never be able to say it enough. "I've missed you so much."

"I've missed you too," came Carla's muffled reply. After a while, her shoulders became still, then she sniffed and sat up, looking around for tissues which she found on the dresser behind her. She grabbed the box and placed it on the couch between them. "I don't really believe Israel is an apartheid state, just so you know."

Lori blew her nose, a little surprised at this turn in the conversation. "I'm glad to hear it. So why . . .?"

"Best way to push your buttons," Carla explained with a shrug.

"Cheeky." Lori gave a watery grin.

"I'll come there, soon. I *do* want to know and understand better and see where and how you live. I really do."

Lori leaned forward and hugged her sister again, then kissed her still damp cheek. "Glad to hear it. We'll be waiting."

"Does Yoni hate me?" Carla asked timidly, wiping her eyes with a tissue.

"No, absolutely not. He just thinks we're both a bit nuts, that's all."

Carla smiled as she took Lori's hands in her own. "This is good."

Lori nodded. "Do you forgive me, Carla?" she whispered.

"Yes, I do, I really do. Do you forgive *me*?" Carla searched her sister's face.

"Absolutely," Lori said softly.

They looked at each other for a few seconds, the night silent apart from Becky's even breathing, Lucy's tiny snuffles, and the whirring of crickets beyond the slightly open window.

"Dad was right," Lori said eventually. "This *is* a choice."

Carla nodded. "Daddy's always right, annoyingly. I've been so busy thinking how wrong you've been that I never allowed myself to think I've also actually been playing a part in all this. But his lecture yesterday morning really hit me. So, I'm choosing to forgive and move on."

Even in the moon-cast shadows, Lori's smile was brilliant. "Me too," she whispered. "New beginnings."

"New beginnings," Carla said with an equally radiant smile, then shook her head. "As easy as that."

"What a couple of idiots we've been," Lori said.

"We could have done this years ago and saved ourselves and everyone else a lot of pain," Carla whispered as she got up to check on the baby.

Assured that all was well with the slumbering Becky and Lucy, Lori and Carla headed to the kitchen for another cup of tea before turning in. Seated at the table with their hands wrapped around the hot mugs, they were able to talk in more than hushed whispers.

"Tell me about Jake, Carla."

"Do I have to?" Carla grimaced.

"Yes, what happened? I don't believe it's over. Jake doesn't give up that easily." She didn't want to tell Carla just yet about her late-night visit to Jake or what he'd said. First, she wanted to hear where Carla stood, to understand what she felt and wanted. And besides, she didn't want to spoil what would definitely be a surprise if Jake proposed.

"I dunno," Carla said, setting her mug down. "I don't know what happened with you two out on the dam, but on the way home he was irritated and tried to talk to me about you. I was being stubborn, as usual, and then he got really mad. Said he couldn't be with anyone who held onto hatred and he was so disappointed with me, and . . ." Carla closed her eyes and shook her head as if trying to dismiss the painful memory.

"And?"

"So, I told him that was too bad, and stormed out the car and into the house." Carla groaned and covered her face with her hands. "How *stupid* can I be?"

Lori put her mug down and squeezed Carla's hand. "It'll work out, I promise."

"I don't think so. I haven't heard from him since then, not so much as a text message even. I think I've really blown it this time."

"Jake's stubborn," Lori said, "but he really loves you, so he's not going to give up on you that easily. He's probably just taken a couple of days to put some distance between you both, so that he can catch his breath."

"Having seen me at my finest hour." Carla rolled her eyes. "Enough to make any man run a mile."

Lori grinned. "I think it's safe to say we've both shown our less-than-pretty sides this holiday."

"Ja, you can say that again. It's been pretty gruesome."

"But nobody's perfect, including Jake. And he'll be alright. You'll both be alright."

"Sorry if I don't share your confidence."

"Do you love him?" Lori was suddenly serious. "Really love him?"

Carla paused, considering the question, then gave a sad smile. "Yes, I do. I really do."

Lori nodded and took another sip. "Then you'll be fine. You'll see, it'll work out."

Carla bit her lip. "But doesn't it bother you?" she asked hesitantly.

"What?"

"Jake and me?"

Lori shook her head. "No, not anymore."

"Can I ask you why it made you so crazy?"

Lori winced. "Was it that obvious?"

"Blatantly." Carla looked concerned. "Are you jealous?"

"Good grief no, not in that way. But you're right, it did make me crazy, if I'm to be brutally honest." She paused and Carla waited. "I tried to analyze it once or twice. It's just . . . it's just . . ." She was annoyed to feel her eyes filling up again. This time it was Carla who reached out and took Lori's hand.

"I'll walk away if you want me to," she whispered.

"Are you kidding? Don't you dare. No, no, it's not what you think." Lori pressed her fingers to her eyes, trying to regain control. "It's just that since Tom . . ." She drew a shuddering breath. "Jake became my substitute brother, I guess. We've kept in really close contact all these years even if we didn't get to meet up very often, and he's very, very important to me."

"Isn't that kind of weird for Yoni?"

"It was a little bit tough for him in the beginning," Lori said, "but he came to understand our friendship for what it is, and in his amazing way, he accepted it."

"Cool guy."

"Yup," Lori agreed. "The very best. I don't know how many men would have put up with me, back then and all these years."

"Jake speaks very highly of Yoni. He really likes him."

"Feeling's mutual, luckily," Lori said. "Anyway, when I saw you and Jake swooning over each other and realized he was behaving like a googly-eyed schoolboy . . ."

"When?" Carla asked.

"My first suspicions were on the drive home from the airport and then tea in the *lapa*, the day Aunt Mae arrived."

"Really?"

Lori nodded and Carla chuckled.

"I didn't think it was funny at the time. It made me furious."

"Ahh, so that's why you stormed off the afternoon Aunt Mae arrived," Carla said. "Jake knew that you weren't happy about us, you know."

"I tried not to show it."

"Hmm, well, here's a news flash: you're not very good at *not* showing your feelings," Carla said. "But I don't understand. If you weren't jealous, then why were you so mad about us?"

Lori looked across the table at Carla. Relieved she could at last speak with stark honesty, she bared her innermost fears. "Because I was afraid I'd lose him too." She held up a hand to hush Carla's protest. She needed to say it all, to slay the giant by bringing it into the light. "You couldn't stand my guts, and I had no doubt Jake would choose you over me. I know he hates conflict and fighting, so he wouldn't have any choice but to shut me out so that he could be with you. And I," her voice broke even though she knew this wasn't a threat any longer, "I would lose another best friend and brother, for the second time."

"Lori . . ." Carla's voice was filled with compassion.

"I know it's irrational but it really filled me with . . . *physical* pain."

Carla shook her head. "He wouldn't, you know."

"Wouldn't what?"

"Choose me over you."

"He would have made us make peace," Lori said. "That's probably why he's gone to town, to get some space so he can make a game plan."

"So, we've beaten him to it," Carla said but her smile quickly faded. "If you're right, and *if* he'll still have me."

"How many times do I have to tell you? He's not going to give up on you that easily, trust me." Lori held up her mug with a celebratory flourish. "To new beginnings, sisterhood and true love."

Carla laughed as she clinked her mug against Lori's. "To corny toasts."

They sipped their tea in silence for a couple of minutes and then Carla frowned again and looked as though she was about to say something.

"What?" Lori asked.

Carla shook her head and smiled back at Lori. "Nothing, nothing at all. Just tired."

As evening began to fall on the day following the storm and Lucy's eventful birth, Jake stopped off at Kalulu. Lori spotted his arrival from the kitchen window and watched him slowly approach the front door, instantly recognizing her friend's uncharacteristic insecurity. Amused yet compassionate, she went out to meet him.

"Hello Jake. Goodness, you look tired."

"I'm on my way back from Lusaka. Bit of a grueling six-hour drive."

"We've had an exciting time while you've been gone."

"I heard, Joe told me. You and Carla are the local heroes," he said.

Lori noticed his eyes looking over her shoulder into the house. "Go on. She's down by the pool."

Jake grinned. "That obvious, huh?"

"Little bit," Lori said as Jake disappeared around the side of the house.

She and Aunt Mae watched from the lounge window as Jake sat on an empty sunbed next to Carla.

"We're spying," Lori said guiltily.

"Oh, come on, just a little bit," Aunt Mae said, grabbing her arm. "Just until we see they're alright."

They didn't have to wait long as after a couple of minutes of seemingly animated discussion, the couple embraced.

"They're okay," Aunt Mae said, turning away with a chuckle.

"Yup, looks like it."

"And you look like the cat that's stolen the cream," Aunt Mae said. "Have you got anything to do with this little make-up?"

"Nothing gets past you, does it, Aunt Mae?" Lori laughed. "I *may* have paid a visit to Jake the evening I went out, after that disastrous church picnic."

"You did good, then," Aunt Mae said, patting Lori's cheek.

"I had to fix what I thought I'd broken. But actually, it wasn't broken at all. Turned out to be a mere miscommunication."

"And your change of heart is nothing short of miraculous, Lori. I'm really proud of you."

"Thank you, Aunt Mae, but it's been a joint effort. As soon as Carla and I made the choice—or perhaps were forced into the choice—to forgive and forget, it all became quite easy. But yes, I'd agree with the idea of a miracle because I seriously never thought it was possible for us to ever even be friends, let alone sisters. And yet here we are. I know you and Mum and Dad have been praying about this for a long time, so . . .

thank you." She reached out and hugged her aunt. "I really appreciate it that you never gave up on us."

"How could we ever give up on you? We knew that given the right time and place, along with a whole lot of love and prayers, you girls would sort yourselves out."

"Ah-ha," Lori said, grinning. "So, this whole birthday thing for Mum really *was* a setup?" She'd already heard as much at Becky's when she'd eavesdropped on the verandah conversation but she couldn't resist teasing her aunt.

"Well now, I . . . I wouldn't call it exactly a setup," Aunt Mae said. "Oh dear, do you mind?"

Lori laughed. "Not at all . . . now. 'Cos it worked, didn't it? You crafty old things. But Mum's going to have to pay the price because she's stuck with having a birthday party, and you know she hates being the center of attention. I guess we'll have to try our best to make it one she'll never forget."

"Oh, I think you've already succeeded in doing that, darling." Aunt Mae tucked her arm through Lori's. "Now let's go see if she needs any help with supper."

Chapter 20

"I can't stop wanting to pinch myself," Beth exclaimed to Mae on that golden-lighted Friday evening as they strolled up the road, "to make sure I'm really awake and it's not all just a lovely dream."

The Maguire household had been permeated with a new and refreshing air of peace and harmony ever since their return from Lusaka a week and a half previously. The house and gardens were once again filled with the sound of laughter and music, causing a puzzled Jonas to ask Beth what had happened. Beth had felt at times as though she would burst with the new and deep sensation of happiness that she'd hardly dared to believe she'd ever feel again.

"I go to sleep every night with a smile on my face like a mad thing. Watch out; you're going to step in the army ants," she warned Mae.

"It *is* rather miraculous," Mae said, making an exaggerated step over the black line of insects marching through the sand. "They really do seem to have put it all behind them and be moving on, haven't they?"

Beth was keeping a slower pace to match Mae and Toffee who were both beginning to puff. Up ahead, Paddy, Lori and Carla strode up the road in the direction of the dip, Rex dashing ahead and then circling back every now and then to ensure Paddy was still going in the same direction.

"Looks like they're all deep in discussion about something," Mae said. "Ooh, look at this line of ants coming up, Beth. That's the biggest I've ever seen. Is Toffee going to be able to make it over?"

"She'll find her way around them," Beth said. "Just don't *you* get bitten, please. Remind me to mention that to Paddy. They look as though they're heading down to the house, so he'll have to tell Fred to keep a good lookout tonight."

"I'm so glad Jake and Carla made up," Aunt Mae said, linking her arm through Beth's. "Do you think they'll get married?"

"Oh, yes," Beth said. "I'd say it's just a matter of time."

"What about her job in Cape Town?"

"She'll have to give that up, won't she? She won't be bored as there's plenty for her to do around here, especially with Jake's new clinic, which'll probably be used by a lot of people in this area."

"She'll want to start a family of her own soon, as well, won't she?" Mae said. "She's nearly thirty."

"That's the way these days, isn't it? Girls think nothing of only starting to plan a family in their thirties, which would have been unthinkable in our day. I know I took a while to have *all* my babies, but I had the twins when I was twenty-five. And even that was considered quite late for first children back then."

They walked on in silence for a few minutes. Beth thought how Mae and John had sadly failed to have any children, but once they'd come to terms with it, they'd filled their lives with each other, their careers and travel. They'd shared many happy years together until the day John had keeled over unexpectedly with a heart attack, leaving her alone. It had been a dreadful shock for Mae, and Beth knew she still missed him terribly.

"Oh, Bethy," Mae exclaimed, stopping in her tracks. "*Look* at that."

The two women stood, arm in arm, looking over the field running next to the sandy single track on which they were walking. The sun was descending in a dazzling blaze behind the hills silhouetted black against the skyline, shooting out rays of light that backlit a scattering of dense white clouds. Gold deepened to the color of liquid lava and then cooled to deep shades of rose and lilac as the fiery ball sank lower.

"Heavenly," Mae said. "How I'll miss these glorious sunsets."

"You don't have to if you don't want to."

Mae turned to look at her sister. "What?"

Beth met her gaze. "You can move out here," she said matter-of-factly. "Come live with us."

"Lori's been talking to you."

"Yes, she mentioned it yesterday when we were having early-morning tea, before you woke up. But Paddy said he'd been thinking the same thing, even before Lori suggested it."

"But I couldn't . . ."

Beth dismissed her as yet unspoken excuses with a wave of her hand and walked on. "Lori said you'd argue that you'd be imposing on us. That's nonsense. You can't impose. You're *family*."

"Rubbish, even if I *am* family."

Beth stopped in her tracks, put her hands on her hips and turned to face Mae.

Mae chuckled. "Now I know where Lori gets it," she said.

Beth ignored her remark and stuck to the point. "My dear Mae, you are my only sister and we are your only family now that John's gone. I want you to come and live with us. I am *asking*, no, *inviting* you to come. And I promise you, you will *not* be imposing."

"But my house . . ."

"You can rent it out."

"And my friends . . ."

"You can go and visit your friends whenever you like," Beth said firmly, now walking a couple of paces ahead of Mae, "but you should *live* close to family."

"What about my medical needs?" Mae panted as she struggled to catch up.

"You're relatively healthy, thankfully, and I guess you'll manage like the rest of us. There are a few good clinics around here and in town, now, you know. And what's more, you can always go back to drizzly old England if you want to, if you're not happy, or you need to, or whatever."

"I don't know, Bethy. It just seems a little crazy, especially at my age."

"Sometimes it's good to be crazy." Beth slowed down and tucked her arm back through Mae's. "Come on, Mae. It'll be fun."

"Paddy will get sick and tired of me," she moaned. "*You'll* get sick and tired of me."

"Never," Beth said. "But I do think Lori's idea of the old cottage is an excellent one. That way, you'll have your own space to retreat to, if you want, when we get on your nerves." She smiled at Mae and squeezed her arm. "We can do it up together. I've been dying to renovate it for ages so now I have a great excuse. It was my first home here, I loved living in it and I'm sure you will too."

"Are you really serious, Beth?"

"Absolutely," Beth said. "We'd love to have you if you could put up with all of us. If it makes it easier for you darling, you can follow the weather—have summers in England and come here when it's winter over there. Whatever works for you. Honestly."

Mae's eyes filled with tears. "I like the sound of that," she said, dabbing a tissue at her eyes. "Ever since John died, I've been afraid of growing old alone. And now, I may not have to." She kissed Beth's cheek and hugged her close. "Thank you, darling. You and Paddy are far too kind."

"You have no idea how happy I'll be not having to say good-bye to you," Beth said sniffling, "wondering when I'll see you again. You'll be doing me the most enormous favor."

"My dearest girl," Mae whispered. "You are something."

"Come on, you two. Less talking, more walking." Paddy grinned at them as he, Lori and Carla strode past them on their way back towards home.

"Tell the night watchman about the ants, please Paddy," Beth called to her husband's retreating back, and he waved his stick above his head in acknowledgment. "Come on, Mae," she said, "let's go home."

The house was quiet and dark. Lori had finished a late-night call but didn't move from the chintz-covered armchair in the corner of her room. She sat in the warm pool of light from the lamp on the nearby dresser, her robe pulled tight around her drawn-up knees, thinking back over the conversation she'd just had with Yoni. She'd told him what they'd been doing over the previous few days, one of the highlights being Ben and Riley's bike-riding competition. The word had spread and it had ended up being quite an event.

"It was such fun," she said. "There were about 20 riders who came with their families. Everyone brought food and drink and it went on till late afternoon. The boys were so chuffed."

"Did the bridge hold up under all that traffic?" Yoni asked, ever practical.

"Yes, well, remember I told you that Joe's team of guys had cleaned it up and fixed it enough so that we could drive home the day after Lucy was born. So, he had a local engineer come and have a look at it a day or two later and I think he had it reinforced before the bike event. But he'll completely rebuild it soon."

"And how are Becky and Lucy?" he asked.

"Becky's fine, tired obviously, but doing great. And Lucy's so gorgeous. Carla and I try and get to see her at least every couple of days."

"It's a big change, this new . . . Carla and you," Yoni said.

Lori was quiet for a little while before answering. "Yes. Yes, it is."

"And it's for real? I mean, it's hard for me to understand and to believe it, you know, from over here."

"Yeah, it's for real. Sometimes it's hard for me to believe the change in both of us. In the end, it was so simple. Crazy, hey? But it's good. I'm really happy."

"I can hear," Yoni said. "You sound different."

"I get why you're a bit confused, but I'll tell you all about it when I come home. Tell me about Jonathan and Noya; how are they?"

They'd chatted for another couple of minutes before ending the call. She understood Yoni's skepticism, but with time, he'd see her new relationship with Carla was real.

Her thoughts wandered to Beth's birthday party. The big day had almost arrived and preparations had reached fever pitch. The four women and Jonas had cooked and baked, stored and frozen, while Paddy and his team of men had set up tables and chairs according to Becky's sketched plans, and laced strings of lights all over the garden. That evening, Paddy had made them stand on the verandah in the dark. Flicking on a switch, he'd chuckled to hear their gasps of delight at the sight of the starry wonderland before them. The desired effect was achieved.

Earlier that afternoon, Carla and Lori had persuaded Aunt Mae to join them for a quick round of croquet in the court they'd made in and around Beth's rose garden.

"I feel like the Queen of Hearts," Aunt Mae had said, "and as though I should be holding an upside-down flamingo instead of a mallet. It's a shame we didn't make this a theme or fancy-dress party."

"No ways Mum would have agreed to that," Carla had said and laughed. "She hates fancy-dress even more than birthday parties."

"Yes, she does, but she might as well be hung for a sheep as a lamb," Aunt Mae had said with a cheeky grin.

Alone in the half-dark, Lori smiled to herself. She'd be taking good memories back home to Israel with her.

She stood up and opened the top drawer of the dresser. Brushing a silk scarf aside, she picked up what had been hidden beneath it. Sitting down again, she tucked her feet under her and carefully lifted the lid of a little blue box to reveal the magnificent lily-shaped diamond ring nestling in its bed of dark velvet. She held it under the lamp, twisting the box this way and that, so the multi-faceted centerpiece sparkled brightly, catching the warm light and scattering its rays in a kaleidoscope of color.

She recalled how little Carla would climb onto Nana's knee and smile up at the grand old lady. "Can you show me how your ring makes rainbows, Nana?" Carla would ask sweetly, and Lily Maguire would smile indulgently and oblige. Delighted by the child's open-mouthed wonder, Lily would let her touch and even hold the precious piece of jewelry.

Lori had always envied Carla's special connection with their grandmother, especially after Tom's death. Little Carla was happiest when her Nana came to stay, which she did for weeks at a time in the latter years of her life.

Not long after Carla's tenth birthday, Lily Maguire was laid to rest next to her husband, on a hill overlooking the great plains in the north of the country where she had so bravely and tirelessly worked to create a home and raise a family, worlds away from her own childhood home and family. Her youngest grand-daughter had been utterly heart-broken for the second time in her short life.

Lori's brow furrowed and she was filled with shame as she remembered a painful scene. Just a couple of weeks after Nana Lily's funeral, it was Lori's last night at home before leaving to go traveling overseas. She had a ticket but beyond that not much of a clue. She was going to go where the breezes blew her, or at least that's what she'd told her worried parents.

Hurting, rebellious, and barely nineteen, Lori had done everything she could to annoy them to the max. Artificially raven-black hair and heavy black make-up were fairly effective, but it was the ring in her nose that had made her father's eye twitch. The piercing had been irritating and uncomfortable, but no ways would she remove it until she was safely on the plane away from what she thought were judging eyes.

On that particular evening she'd been lolling on the couch, giving monosyllabic answers to her father's persistent questions about her upcoming trip and life plans in general, until he'd quietly left the room.

Finally, she'd thought triumphantly, he's given up. But she'd been wrong.

A few minutes later, Paddy had come back into the lounge holding something in his hand. He came over to where she lounged and held out the small object. Rolling her eyes and with an exaggerated sigh, she'd turned to look, expecting him to be offering her some university pamphlets or perhaps religious literature for her to take with her on her travels. Instead, what she saw on the flat of his rough hand had made her suck in her breath and sit straight up.

Sitting down beside her, he'd said simply, "Here, take it. It's yours."

Lori had stared at him, her mouth literally hanging open. "What? Why?"

"According to Maguire family tradition, your Nana's ring should have gone to Tom as the eldest son to give to his wife. But . . . so . . . it's yours. And I'm *trusting* you to look after it and—even more importantly—to look after yourself."

"I . . . I . . ." Lori had stuttered. All her tough teenage bravado had evaporated as her shaky black-tipped fingers reached out towards the beautiful heirloom. Before she could touch it, the air was split by a heart-rending scream.

"Daddy, no!" Carla had leapt up from where she'd been reading and lunged at her father, her eyes wild and face ashen. "You can't, you can't give it to her, it's mine," she'd cried, pummeling his knees in anguish.

Lori had quickly snapped the little blue box shut and held it in a tight fist behind her back. "Why on earth would you think it's yours?"

Carla was distraught and almost incoherent. "Be . . . because Nana knew I . . . I . . . she said, Daddy, please. Lori won't love it like I do. Daddy, *please*," she'd sobbed.

"Too bad, little girl," Lori had sneered at Carla in one of her uglier moments. "You can't always get everything you want, not even by throwing a tantrum."

She'd stalked out the room, clutching the box and grinning as Carla wailed broken-heartedly behind her. Sweet victory, she'd told herself, determinedly squashing the niggling in the pit of her stomach that uncomfortably felt more like guilt than triumph.

"I'm sorry, Nana Lily," the older, wiser and remorseful Lori now whispered, gently closing the little blue box. "I promise I'll make it right."

She placed it back in the drawer, covered it with the silk scarf, and went to bed.

The day of the party, Lori begged off the morning run. "You go ahead," she said drowsily to Carla who was standing, dressed and ready to go, at Lori's door. "I'll give it a miss this morning. Had a late night."

"Lazy bones," Carla said, and closed the door behind her.

As soon as Carla had gone, Lori threw back the covers and sat up. Folding the swathes of mosquito net back onto its frame, she pulled on her robe and padded out barefoot to the bathroom. Ten minutes later, she was dressed and making her way down the long passageway toward Paddy's office on the far side of the quad. His large desk, another one of Benson's beautiful creations, was strategically positioned so he could look out of one window to the quad on his right, and out of the other to the workshops on his left.

"Morning Daddy."

Paddy looked up with surprise as Lori walked in. "Hello darling," he said, removing his glasses. "You didn't go out with Carla for a run this morning?"

"No," Lori said, gazing at the collection of framed photographs on the wall opposite his desk. "Actually, I'd like to talk to you, if you don't mind." She turned back to face him. "Can we take our tea out to Tom's garden?"

"Everything alright?" Paddy asked with concern.

"Yes, fine. Just want to chat a bit."

"Okay, sure," Paddy said, pushing back his chair to stand up. "Let's go make us a couple of mugs and we can take them out."

"Perfect."

A short while later, they were sitting side by side on the bench in the hedged garden just beyond the homestead fence. A flock of tiny birds were chirping their delight with the new day, fluttering around in a flurry of activity.

"You wouldn't think that a graveside could be called a 'happy place' but this is definitely one of mine," Lori said after a few minutes. "It's so serene and pretty."

"Your mother keeps it looking beautiful, all year around."

"Tom would love it."

Paddy nodded, but didn't speak. Lori set her mug down beside her on the bench and reached into her jacket pocket. Drawing out the little blue box, she offered it to Paddy on her open palm, much as he had done to her all those years ago.

Paddy stared at the box without speaking and then slowly reached out a slightly shaking hand to take it from her. He opened the box, removed the ring from its bed of velvet and twisted it, this way and that. Eventually, he turned a teary smile to Lori.

"Don't make me cry, Dad," Lori said.

He shook his head. "Don't mind me. It just brought your Nana back to me for a minute," he said, carefully putting the ring back in its box.

"I've never worn it, Daddy," Lori said gently. Paddy didn't answer, so she continued. "I knew in my heart it never really belonged to me. In fact, I know that Nana would've much preferred to have blown family tradition and given it to Carla. I knew it back then as well, I just didn't want to admit it. All the same, I could never bring myself to even *try* and wear it. Instead, I just kept it safe. I had it insured and I've been keeping it under lock and key ever since."

"Why did you bring it here, Lori?" Paddy asked, looking confused. "It should go to Jonathan to give to his wife one day, if you don't want it."

Lori shook her head. "No, Daddy. It belongs to Carla," she said firmly. "Nana always wanted her to have it."

Paddy was quiet for a long minute and then asked, "Are you going to give it to her?"

"No," Lori said, and Paddy looked even more baffled. "No, Dad. I want you to give it to Jake to give to

Carla as an engagement ring. If you agree, of course. It was your mother's ring so I think this is your decision."

Paddy didn't speak. He just stared at her for so long that Lori mistook his silence for disapproval and tried to reinforce her position.

"I'm sorry about the family tradition, Daddy, but I'm convinced it's the right thing to do, and I'm sure Tom would've agreed. He would've wanted it this way."

Suddenly she realized Paddy wasn't angry or disappointed. He was simply lost for words.

"Your Nana and Tom would've been very, very proud of you, my girl," he said eventually, his voice gruff with emotion. "But no one more than me. You blow me away."

Lori smiled through her own tears. "I only wish I'd done this years ago."

"Now seems like perfect timing to me. I have a feeling Jake won't wait long before proposing, so perhaps Nana's ring will give him a wee nudge in the right direction," Paddy said with a conspiratorial wink.

"I hope so," Lori said.

Chapter 21

Beth couldn't have wished for more perfect weather. The grey clouds that had hovered the previous day had vanished, leaving behind them powder-blue skies, warm sunshine and a soft breeze.

She did a final round of house and garden. The roses she'd cut before breakfast filled the lobby and lounge with their scent. Lori had laid the large, round tables set out around the pool area with white linen cloths and polished silverware and glasses, while Carla created centerpieces of cream roses and delicate greenery wrapped around large white candles. The hot buffet dinner would be set out on the long tables running along one inside wall of the *lapa*, but now they were set for afternoon tea. Beth was satisfied that all was ready.

Becky, Joe and family were the first to arrive just before midday, with Jake just a few minutes behind them. Beth had asked him to join them for a snack lunch and he was keen to help with anything that still needed doing. But there was nothing much left to do and Jake seemed happy to sit and hold baby Lucy for a while instead. She opened her grey-blue eyes and stared at him solemnly as he cradled her gently in the crook of his arm.

"Suits you, Hamilton," Lori said.

"You've done it this time, Becks," he said. "She's a heartbreaker."

"Come on everybody," Beth said. "We've all got to go and get changed and ready. People will be arriving soon."

"Shouldn't be here before four," Paddy said.

"Well, it's nearly three now."

"Jake, you, Joe and the boys can use my room," Carla said. "Becky and I will be with Lori."

The three sisters disappeared into Lori's bedroom to dress and do each other's make-up, emerging an hour later to join the others.

Beth gasped when she saw them and hugged each of them in turn. "*Thank* you for dressing up like this and making it all so special for me."

"It hasn't even begun," Becky said.

"It's already so much more than I dreamed possible, because of you girls."

"Mum, please don't start," Carla said. "You'll set us all off bawling, bunch of cry-babies that we are."

Promptly at four o'clock, the sound of a car heralded the arrival of their first guests, Hugh and Rose. Fred waved them into the designated parking area by the workshops with exaggerated gestures as Paddy strode out to meet them. They were soon followed by a string of other vehicles, all signaled by Fred's pantomime to find their allotted parking spots.

"Look how beautiful you all are!" Rose exclaimed with admiration as Beth and her daughters came forward to greet her.

The guests continued to arrive over the next hour or so. "Africa time," Paddy said, noticing Mae's disapproving expression as the final car drew in after five o'clock.

"It would drive me mad," she said, checking to see if there was still enough hot water for the late arrivals' tea.

"No, it's not a problem. They might have a good reason, like something urgent to do on their farm, or a puncture on the way, or whatever."

"Who are you and what have you done with my brother-in-law, Mr. Punctuality?"

"Ah, the trick is to keep your own standards, Mae, no matter what everyone else is doing. But anyway, I hear you're going to have to get used to our Africa time," Paddy said with a wink.

Mae's smile faded into a worried frown. "Are you okay with that, Paddy? You can tell me if you're not, you know. It wasn't my idea anyway, so I won't be offended."

"Beth's ecstatic about the idea, and whatever makes Beth happy is alright with me," he replied, meeting her gaze evenly. "Ah good, it's Chanda Solomon, our doctor and his wife." He strode off to meet his latest guests.

"Okay, then," Mae whispered to herself.

"What are you muttering to yourself about?" Beth appeared at her elbow.

"Just checking hot water and the like," Mae said with a quick smile. "I'd better go and top up the milk jug. The doctor's just arrived, apparently."

"Yes, I saw. I'll introduce you. They're a lovely couple, originally from Lusaka. She had a hard time settling in away from the city, poor dear, but she loves it here now. Hello Thandi! So glad you could come. Meet my sister . . ."

Lori sat alone in one of the cushioned wicker chairs set under a tree in a lower corner of the garden, close to where she'd seen the monkeys crossing. She'd kicked off her sandals and with one hand was gently rocking the pram standing beside her, every now and then peeking under its covering net to check on the sleeping Lucy. She relished this quiet break after all the busyness and emotion of the past few weeks. And besides, it gave her an opportunity to people-watch, which she loved.

Gales of laughter from the rose garden indicated another round of croquet was underway. Lawn croquet played Maguire-family-style was far from the sedate game politely enjoyed in other parts of the world, but no doubt much more fun, Lori thought. She and Carla had already taken on Jake and Joe in a hilarious game that had ended in elated victory for the sisters, despite the men's blatant cheating.

To her left, the *lapa* was full of people either playing ping-pong and billiards or sitting and chatting at the bar or in the comfy chairs spread around. Ben, Riley, and their friends were making the most of the swimming pool. Soon, the temperature would drop together with the sun and they'd have to be persuaded to get dried and dressed. They'd be having pizzas and kid-friendly movies that evening, while the adults had dinner outside.

The sky was slowly turning to burnished copper, a magnificent sunset in honor of the occasion. Lori snapped some photos of the scenes around her with her phone and sent them to Yoni. If only he and the children had been here with her, this would all have been utterly perfect. Tiny mewing sounds from beneath the mosquito net covering the pram interrupted her thoughts.

"Hello beautiful," she cooed as she stood up and lifted the baby out, quickly wrapping her in a fleecy blanket. "Shall we go find your Mum?"

As she looked around to see where Becky was, Lori spotted Paddy, Beth, and Jake standing and talking together on the verandah. As she watched, Beth reached up and embraced Jake; then she turned and headed down the lawn to the *lapa* while Paddy and Jake disappeared into the lounge.

"Good for you," Lori whispered, confident she knew the subject of Jake's conversation with her parents, and why Paddy had taken Jake into the house. He was probably escorting him to his office for a man-to-man chat and hopefully presentation of a certain precious heirloom.

Kissing Lucy's soft baby cheeks, Lori continued to coo, "Good for him, hey Luce?"

"Good for who?"

Startled, Lori turned to see both Becky and Carla standing close behind her, Becky reaching for her baby.

"When did she wake up?" asked Becky.

Lori, relieved they weren't going to insist on an answer, handed Lucy over.

"Just a couple of minutes ago; she had a lovely sleep."

"Great, thanks. I'll take her in for a feed."

"Feel free to use my room, if we haven't left it in too much of a mess," Lori said. "Carla, let's take all the tea things inside and see if there's anything left to do before dinner."

"Sure." Carla matched her stride to Lori's as they headed for the *lapa*. "Good for who?"

"Huh?" Lori tried playing dumb.

"You were saying, 'good for him'. Good for who?"

"Um . . . eh . . . good for Dad," Lori stammered. "Good for Dad for making all this happen for Mum. So much for her disliking parties and being made a fuss of—looks like she's loving it all."

"I know," Carla said. "She looks really happy. It's good to see her like this."

Lori nodded, silently congratulating herself on dodging an awkward bullet as she began loading used tea cups and mugs onto an empty tray.

The Maguire's guests enjoyed their meal in the soft glow of the table candles and the strings of tiny lights zig-zagging across the whole garden. More candles had been lit and set to float all over the pool in water-lily holders—a gift from Carla one Christmas past—with magical effect.

Once coffee and desserts had been served, Paddy called for glasses to be refilled as he stood to make his speech.

"As we look around our home and garden tonight, Beth and I see how incredibly blessed we are. We consider ourselves immeasurably wealthy in having all of you in our lives. You are our great friends and neighbors in the very best sense. Like a big family, we've all shared each other's joys and sorrows, successes and hardships, over the years, haven't we?" Heads all around the tables nodded in solemn agreement. "That's the kind of wealth that the ups and downs of politics and shaky economies can't take away.

"Sometimes, in our own homes and families, acceptance and forgiveness can be the most difficult. But for the grace of God . . ." Paddy paused and the splashing of the pool's waterfall was thrown into sharp relief by the silence. "Tonight, I thank God for His gift to me of my precious family, for His gracious faithfulness that has carried us through the years, and the healing power of *His* forgiveness. So, please raise your glasses and join me in toasting my soul-mate and the love of my life, my wonderful wife Beth, who I must say is looking especially lovely tonight."

Turning to Beth, his wine glass outstretched toward her, Paddy's eyes were teary as he said, "Bethy, my darling, you gave up so much to marry me and you've never stopped giving—four wonderful children, our beautiful home and so much more. Happy birthday, sweetheart, and I pray we'll share many, *many* more together." He bent to kiss her upturned face and then raised his glass. "To Beth."

"To Beth," everyone called out in unison.

"And to Lucy," Beth said, dabbing her tears with a napkin.

Paddy raised his glass again. "Indeed, a very special welcome to the newest member of the Maguire clan, our beautiful granddaughter Lucy."

"Great speech, Daddy. You succeeded in making us all cry," Lori said as she hugged Paddy and then turned to Beth. "Happy birthday, Mum."

Lori signaled Jake and they both headed into the *lapa*.

"Mum, Dad," she called, "it's time to show us all how it's done. Come on down here, please. The song that's about to be played is Mum and Dad's wedding song, from *way* back when."

"Hey, watch it," Paddy said.

Lori held up a hand to stay his remarks and the resulting laughter. "My brother, sisters and I grew up on this song. Dad would put it on our old record-player and we'd all waltz around like they did. But sometimes, they didn't even need the music. I remember occasions when we were camping out in the middle of the bush; us kids would peep out our tents to watch these two love-birds dancing around the campfire as they *hummed* the tune . . ."

"You were *supposed* to be sleeping," Beth said amidst more laughter.

"Seriously, you two have never stopped dancing together, and we love you and thank you for that. What an amazing example you've been to all of us. So now, ladies and gentlemen," Lori said with mock solemnity, "without further ado, I give you Beth and Paddy Maguire from . . . 1975."

Amidst hoots and cheers and in perfect timing to the soulful melody, Paddy took Beth's hand and twirled her around the floor.

"*Let's stay together,*" he crooned, making Beth giggle self-consciously.

First Joe and Becky and then Jake and Carla joined them on the dance floor, while Lori dropped into a chair next to Aunt Mae.

"Who'd have thought?" she said. "Mum's actually enjoying being the center of attention for a change. What a couple of rock-stars she and Dad are."

"You girls certainly pulled it off," Aunt Mae said. "It's a great party."

Lori and Carla had prepared a play-list that kept the dance-floor filled until well past midnight when the last guests disappeared up the driveway, some with their slumbering children loaded onto the back seat of their vehicles. Paddy, Beth and Lori waved them off before going back down to the *lapa* to join Carla and Aunt Mae.

"I used to love it when you two would stay out late and Tom and I would be put to sleep in someone's bedroom," Lori said. "When it was time to go, you'd carry us out to the car and we'd pretend to still be asleep. We'd lie there on the back seat and watch the moon and the stars race us home."

Mae smiled at Lori tenderly. "That's a sweet memory."

"Little monkeys," Paddy said with a chuckle. "You thought we couldn't hear your whispering and giggling. Come on, let's go to bed," he said and yawned. "We can tidy up in the morning."

They blew out the remaining candle stubs and strolled up to the house together.

"You must be tired, Dad," Lori said. "You always used to make us clean everything up before letting us go to bed."

"That was then. Now I'm old, so I say we'll get a good night's sleep and attack it with some help tomorrow."

"I gave Jonas the day off tomorrow." Beth matched Paddy's yawn. She looked tired, but happy.

"Good," Paddy said. "He deserves it. Did a sterling job. I believe Jake is coming over for the day, so I'm sure he'll help me get the lights down and do any other heavy work."

"Joe'll be here as well," Beth said. "He and Becks will be back for the day as it's Lori's last one here, but I'd prefer to have things tidy by the time they come otherwise Becky will start dashing around doing things, and I don't want that."

Lori embraced Beth in a warm hug. "Did you enjoy your party, Mum?"

Beth took Lori's face in her hands. "So much more than I'd dared to imagine," she said.

Chapter 22

Lori woke very early to a Sunday morning quiet. She was tired but as this was her last day, she didn't want to waste it sleeping. She washed and dressed, made herself tea and took it out into the garden to sit by the pool, grateful to watch the tail end of a beautiful sunrise.

Draining her cup, she began to look around at the aftermath of the previous night's party. It had been a roaring success, which justified the mess that had been left behind. It was very uncharacteristic of their family to leave it until morning but they'd all been very tired. It wouldn't have happened if Becky had stayed till the end, Lori thought.

By the time the rest of the family woke up, Lori had tidied the pool area and lounge, leaving only the heavy lifting to the men. Sad about having to leave her family and Kalulu, she was grateful to be busy. She'd just finished drying the last stack of clean dishes in Beth's kitchen when Paddy came in to make the morning tea.

"Sweetheart, you've been busy," he said.

"Hmm, last day blues so I've been glad of the distraction. Your tray's ready over there and the kettle's about to boil."

"Thank you darling," Paddy said giving her a comforting squeeze. "Now leave those dishes and come have tea with us."

Lori followed Paddy to her parents' bedroom and settled down next to her mother, ready to enjoy a second cup of tea. As the three of them chatted and laughed about the events of the evening before, they were joined first by Aunt Mae and then a sleepy looking Carla.

"You all woke me up," Carla said. "Move over." She feigned grumpiness as she puffed the pillows and curled up next to Lori.

"I should think so," Paddy said. "It's very late."

"No timetable today, Dad," she mumbled. "You promised."

"Well, you'll be glad to hear your sister has done most of the tidying up already, so you can have a lazier morning than you expected."

Carla's eyes flew open and she looked up at Lori. "Seriously? Why didn't you wait for me? You didn't need to do it all on your own."

"Last day blues."

"Hmm, I know those."

Lori changed the subject. "What's the plan for today, Mum?"

"We're just going to have a quiet day at home, sweetheart. Brunch with Becks and Joe when they arrive, and I invited Jake too, of course. And then later we can have a *braai* by the pool, if that's what we feel like."

"Sounds perfect," Lori said, handing her empty tea-cup to her mother to set down on her bedside table. "It'd be nice to take a walk to the dam this afternoon too, if you're all up to it."

"Whatever you want, darling," Beth said giving her a hug. "It's your day."

As usual, the day passed far too quickly for Lori. While she was excited to think she'd be seeing Yoni, Jonathan, and Noya again, she couldn't get rid of the lump in her throat. It was always the same on her last day at Kalulu: tears close to the surface, her mind desperately storing up mental snapshots and shooting arrow prayers: "Lord, help me see them all again; let me come back here again."

All very pessimistic, but she couldn't help it. Just as she was hesitant about leaving her home in Israel to make the trip to Zambia, so now her inner child curled up and cried within her at the thought of leaving her childhood home and family. But she kept all this to herself so as not to spoil the day for everyone else.

In the late afternoon, the family set off down the path through the bush to the dam.

"Walk with me, Lor," Jake said coming alongside Lori. "I want you to myself for a bit."

They walked briskly ahead, easily putting a comfortable distance between them and the rest of the family party.

"It's been great to see you," Jake said after a few minutes' silence.

"You too," Lori said. "Please come visit us soon. It'd be really nice to see you more often than just once every two or three years."

Jake was quiet again as they walked on through the bush, eventually coming out into the opening and down to the wide dam wall.

"I'm going to propose to her, Lor."

Lori's stride didn't falter; she merely smiled up at him and tucked her arm through his.

"I know, Jake, and I'm glad. Thanks for telling me first, though, I appreciate that."

"Well, not exactly first," Jake said a bit sheepishly. "I spoke to your parents last night."

"I know, I saw."

Jake laughed. "Does nothing ever get past you?"

"Hmm, no, not much."

"Anyway, I wanted to tell you; I wanted you to know, before I ask her."

"Thanks, and . . . I'm glad." Lori smiled up at him, amazed to find she really was very happy about it.

As the sun set, the family prepared for an early supper in the *lapa*. Joe and Jake tended to the barbecue while Paddy opened a couple of bottles of wine left over from the previous evening. Nature's orchestra of crickets, frogs, and nightjars provided the musical backdrop. The floating candles were relit and Lori agreed with

Ben and Riley that the pool was the prettiest ever created.

As they ate, the conversation turned to current affairs in Israel. They hadn't spoken about it again since the day of the church picnic, but now the discussion raised no tension.

"I'd like to come and visit you there," Carla said tentatively, "sometime soon."

Lori was thrilled. "We'd love that," she said. "You're more than welcome, any time."

"Well," Paddy said, "Your mother and I have never stopped praying for peace in our family. It's taken a good many years but it's finally become a reality. So, you can be sure we won't stop praying for peace in your part of the world especially, Lori. And if I didn't say it before, I'll say it now: I'm really proud of you girls."

"Thank you, Daddy," Lori and Carla said in unison.

Jake stood up and cleared his throat. "I'd like to say something, if you don't mind." Looking toward Paddy, he waited until the Maguire patriarch, already so like a father to him, nodded his approval before continuing.

"As you all know, Lori has always been the pain in my neck." He grinned at her mock scowl. "But she's also been the very best friend any man could wish for. So, before she goes back to where she belongs, I wanted to say thank you. You have all been such a huge part of my life, from the day I was born I guess, and I've always thought of you as my extended family." He paused and took a deep breath. "So, I'd like to make the connection official."

Carla's eyes were wide with surprise as Jake came over to where she sat, taking both her hands in his own.

"Carla Maguire, this may seem a bit soon after we kind of went public, but you know I've loved you for years. I can't see you get on another plane without knowing when you're coming back. I'm pretty sure you feel the same way, so . . ." He took another deep breath and dropped to one knee. "Will you marry me?"

Carla didn't hesitate. "Yes, a thousand times yes!" she cried.

"Right answer," Jake said to the amusement of the teary-eyed onlookers, as he drew the little box out of his pocket.

Carla froze as he gently opened it to reveal the lily-shaped ring nestled in blue velvet.

She gasped and flashed a questioning look at Lori who simply smiled back at her and nodded encouragingly.

"Woman, do you want the ring or don't you?" Jake asked with feigned exasperation.

"I . . . I don't understand, but yes, I do, I do!"

He slid the ring onto her finger and they kissed as Paddy popped open the large bottle of champagne he'd ferreted away after his private conversation with Jake. Glasses were filled and tearful congratulations, hugs and kisses were given all round.

Carla came and stood in front of Lori. "I'm so sorry I was such an ass for so many years," she said.

"I was probably the bigger ass, and I'm sorry too, for all the wasted time," Lori said. "But that's all behind us now."

"Nana's ring," Carla said questioningly. "I don't understand. Why . . ."

Lori lifted Carla's left hand and caressed the exquisite piece of jewelry that sparkled on her ring finger. "It's what Nana would have wanted, and Tom. Look how perfectly it fits, and it's far more beautiful on you than it would be on me or anyone else." She paused and then looked into her sister's beautiful, tear-filled eyes. "It's never been mine, Carla; it's always been yours. That's why I couldn't bring myself to ever wear it. I'm sorry I was so mean. I should never have taken it from Dad all those years ago, but it's back where it belongs now."

"Thank you," Carla whispered, hugging Lori. "Thank you."

"You're welcome, Sis."

"I'll take good care of them both."

"I'm sure you will. But always remember no matter how valuable and beautiful Nana's ring is, the real treasure you've gained today is Jake."

"I know," Carla said, her lips curled in a dreamy smile. "I know."

The inevitable parting came all too soon. An early-morning snack breakfast in Beth's kitchen followed by lingering, tearful goodbyes. Jake and Carla had offered to drive Lori to the airport. He loaded her luggage into the back of his jeep and climbed into the driver's seat, tactfully leaving the family to say their goodbyes.

This time, Lori insisted on traveling in the back seat and after last hugs with Beth, Paddy and Aunt Mae, she climbed up, jammed sunglasses over her eyes and busied herself checking her bag for passport and ticket.

Jake drove through the gate and away as Lori stared out the window at a blurred collage of familiar fields and trees. Before they turned onto the main road, Lori looked back for a last glimpse of the long red road leading down to the Maguire homestead. With a deep sigh, she dried her tears and settled a small pillow between the window and her head. She was tired.

A couple of hours later, Jake pulled into the airport parking lot and found a space. An attendant, eager for a tip, rushed to meet the car with a luggage trolley and preceded them into the small unlikely-looking bungalow that was the departure hall. It was surprisingly informal, and after checking in Lori was able to come back through the glass doors to have a drink with Jake and Carla until boarding time.

"Be sure to tell Yoni and the kids we want to see them at our wedding," Jake said, and Lori nodded.

"Where do you think you'll have it?" she asked.

"I guess at home, don't you think, Jake?" Carla said.

"It worked well for Mum's party," Lori said, "so you can do something like that or step it up a notch. And I guess the next big question is when."

"We'll keep you posted," Carla said. "We haven't had a chance to talk about it yet."

"When do you fly back to Cape Town?"

"Mid-week," Carla said. "I messaged Max last night, so he knows what's coming."

"When do you think you'll leave work and move up?"

"Not sure, we haven't talked about that yet either."

"Of course not." Lori sipped her drink and tried to keep her mind focused on the small talk rather than her departure.

A bored-sounding and barely understandable voice announced over the intercom that it was time for all passengers flying to Johannesburg to board. Lori stood, swung her bag over her shoulder, and hugged Jake for a long minute. He kissed the top of her head, but neither of them spoke.

She turned to Carla whose eyes were awash with tears.

"We can do this, Carla. Mum and Aunt Mae have managed a great long-distance relationship, all these years, so we can do it too. Like we have with Becky. We just have to build on that. And I'll be waiting for your visit. Come soon, okay?"

They hugged wordlessly for a long time until Lori kissed Carla's cheek and then turned quickly to walk past the security guard and to the back of the small hall. Standing in the queue, boarding pass at the ready, she heard Carla shout her name.

"Lori!"

Lori turned to look back at Carla where she stood by the security guard, her face now streaming with tears.

"Who was it, Lor?"

Lori raised her hands in a questioning gesture.

"In my dream—when I'm underwater and being pulled up. It was more than a dream, wasn't it? Who saved me?"

Lori shook her head. "It doesn't matter, Carla."

"It was you," Carla said with a small sob. It was a statement, not a question.

Lori tried to smile and waved. Covering her eyes with her sunglasses, she quickly turned and went out into the bright sunlight, crossing the tarmac towards the plane.

The choking lump in Lori's throat finally had the better of her and morphed into hot tears, filling her eyes then spilling down her cheeks. She let them run and fall, unchecked, not caring who saw. She stared out of the small oval window at the wing of the plane, at its bolts and lettering, 'DO NOT WALK OUTSIDE THIS AREA', with a missing 'I'.

At the far edge of the tarmac a large white helicopter was parked, the colors of the flag on its tail below the rotor and 'ZAMBIA AIR FORCE' painted on its side. Beyond stood a ramshackle of barn-type buildings surrounded by a cluster of trees of different shapes and sizes, and browning grass, as tall as a man.

Lori's tears and racing thoughts had stopped as she'd concentrated on all these details, but suddenly she caught sight of Carla and Jake standing on the other side of the tall fence bordering the tarmac, and both started afresh.

"My life of goodbyes," she whispered softly as her vision blurred again. She pressed the palm of her hand to the window as if to touch them again and wondered if they could see her through the tiny window.

The ache squeezing her heart was a physical pain. She was vaguely aware of the safety instruction film showing on the small screen above the seat in front of her, but her eyes remained fixed on the dusty scene outside. The engines started to hum in an ever-increasing crescendo and she felt the vibrations through her seat. The small screens disappeared into the overhead panels, and the captain instructed the cabin crew to be seated. The engines roared as the plane shuddered and moved, at first slowly until it turned onto its allotted runway and then faster and faster.

"Underneath are the Everlasting Arms," Lori whispered, finding comfort in her mother's customary pre-flight prayer as the plane lifted off the ground.

She stared down at the brown grass meeting the blue-grey horizon and greyish sky above as if to imprint the essence of the land on her memory, until it disappeared from view, far below the rising plane. She heard the *rrr-clunk* as the wheels were withdrawn and tucked in. The plane bucked and swayed, circled on its right wing, giving her a last glimpse of the brown ground dotted with miniature, square brick houses and dark green trees, before it straightened, quickly climbed above the clouds and levelled, its course set for the two-hour flight south.

Lori's tears had dried although the ache was still there and she felt numb. She was going back to Yoni and the children, which was good—she'd missed them terribly—but a large part of her heart would always belong to this corner of Africa. It was there, in the land of her birth, and of her father's and his father before her, that she felt most settled, belonging, even after all these years away.

She sipped the iced juice she'd received from the air hostess and relaxed against the head-rest. This time her leaving felt different. At the core of her heartache there was a new sense of deep peace and joy, the result of past wrongs and conflicts put to right. It was as though a locked door in her heart had been broken open and soothing, healing light was pouring into the darkness behind it.

She closed her eyes and smiled, hearing Paddy's voice in her head as clearly as if he was sitting beside her: "Family is God's love to us through one another."

It had taken almost all her life, but at last, she understood.

Epilogue

"A sister is a gift to the heart, a friend to the spirit, a golden thread to the meaning of life."

Isadora James

Lori stood against the barrier in the high-ceilinged arrivals hall of Ben Gurion airport, near Tel Aviv. Her fingers drummed the cold steel impatiently, her eyes fixed on the tall doors sliding open and shut as they discharged an assortment of travelers. It had been a long time in the planning, but at last, her whole family were coming to visit.

As she and Yoni waited, Lori thought back over some of the events of the previous year. She had made the trip with Yoni, Jonathan and Noya to Kalulu in the December following Beth's birthday party for Carla and Jake's wedding. For the second time that year, the Maguire garden had been transformed, even more beautifully than for Beth's party.

Carla had predictably made a breathtakingly beautiful bride and when she appeared on the verandah, her arm linked through Paddy's, there had been gasps and murmurs of appreciation from the guests. It had been a happy and fun celebration, made even more special for the Maguires because Jake's parents had journeyed out from the States for the occasion. The speeches had made everyone laugh and cry, and the dancing had continued into the small hours of the morning.

Now, fifteen months later, it was late spring in Israel, Lori's favorite time of year. The weather was perfect before the heat of summer, the hills and fields covered with multi-colored carpets of wild flowers.

Impatient for them to appear, Lori thought about the different things she'd planned for them all to do: beach picnics and rock pool explorations along the coast where they lived, the dawn Easter service at the Garden Tomb outside the Old City walls in Jerusalem, a boat ride on the Sea of Galilee . . .

The sliding doors shunted open and there they were.

"Yoni, they're here," she said, waving to attract their attention before running toward them.

They had all come. Joe carried two-year old Lucy, her head of golden curls lolling against his shoulder in tiredness from the long, night flight. A taller-looking Ben and Riley jostled as they pushed a case-laden trolley together. Jake pushed a second loaded trolley alongside Beth, Paddy and Aunt Mae. And there were her sisters, waving elatedly back at her: Becky, slim and sporting a shorter hairstyle; Carla, five months pregnant and blooming.

"I can't believe you're all here," Lori cried, not bothering to wipe away her tears of happiness as she embraced them all.

There would be more goodbyes, as always, but for now, she'd rejoice in the sweet hellos.

CPSIA information can be obtained
at www.ICGtesting.com
Printed in the USA
LVHW050957160419
614334LV00004B/528